Other books by this author available from New English Library:

EDGE 1: THE LONER
EDGE 2: TEN THOUSAND DOLLARS AMERICAN
EDGE 3: APACHE DEATH
EDGE 4: KILLER'S BREED
EDGE 5: BLOOD ON SILVER
EDGE 6: THE BLUE, THE GREY AND THE RED
EDGE 7: CALIFORNIA KILLING
EDGE 8: SEVEN OUT OF HELL
EDGE 9: BLOODY SUMMER
EDGE 10: VENGEANCE IS BLACK
EDGE 11: SIOUX UPRISING
EDGE 12: THE BIGGEST BOUNTY
EDGE 13: A TOWN CALLED HATE
EDGE 14: THE BIG GOLD
EDGE 15: BLOOD RUN
EDGE 16: THE FINAL SHOT
EDGE 17: VENGEANCE VALLEY
EDGE 18: TEN TOMBSTONES TO TEXAS
EDGE 19: ASHES AND DUST
EDGE 20: SULLIVAN'S LAW
EDGE 21: RHAPSODY IN RED
EDGE 22: SLAUGHTER ROAD
EDGE 23: ECHOES OF WAR
EDGE 24: THE DAY DEMOCRACY DIED
EDGE 25: VIOLENCE TRAIL
EDGE 26: SAVAGE DAWN
EDGE 27: DEATH DRIVE
EDGE 28: EVE OF EVIL
EDGE 29: THE LIVING, THE DYING AND THE DEAD
EDGE 30: TOWERING NIGHTMARE
EDGE 31: THE GUILTY ONES

ADAM STEELE 1: THE VIOLENT PEACE
ADAM STEELE 2: BOUNTY HUNTER
ADAM STEELE 3: HELL'S JUNCTION
ADAM STEELE 4: VALLEY OF BLOOD
ADAM STEELE 5: GUN RUN
ADAM STEELE 6: THE KILLING ART
ADAM STEELE 7: CROSS-FIRE
ADAM STEELE 8: COMANCHE CARNAGE
ADAM STEELE 9: BADGE IN THE DUST
ADAM STEELE 10: THE LOSERS
ADAM STEELE 11: LYNCH TOWN
ADAM STEELE 12: DEATH TRAIL
ADAM STEELE 13: BLOODY BORDER
ADAM STEELE 14: DELTA DUEL
ADAM STEELE 15: RIVER OF DEATH
ADAM STEELE 16: NIGHTMARE AT NOON
ADAM STEELE 17: SATAN'S DAUGHTERS
ADAM STEELE 18: THE HARD WAY
ADAM STEELE 19: THE TARNISHED STAR
ADAM STEELE 20: WANTED FOR MURDER

WAGONS EAST

George G. Gilman

NEW ENGLISH LIBRARY/TIMES MIRROR

for
BILL and WIN
in appreciation of their art.

A New English Library Original Publication, 1979

First NEL Paperback Edition June 1979

NEL Books are published by
New English Library from
Barnard's Inn, Holborn,
London EC1N 2JR.
Made and printed in Great Britain by
C. Nicholls & Company Ltd
The Philips Park Press, Manchester.

45004282 0

CHAPTER ONE

THE RAIN stopped lashing at the roof and north facing wall of the timber shack and the man who had been sheltering in the place pulled open the creaking door and stood on the threshold: listening to the diminishing sound of the wind and peering out over the pine forest that filled the valley below. The valley cut a deep indentation in the Blue Mountains of Oregon, running south east from the slope on which the shack was perched. And it was in that direction that the wind had veered to push the heavy, drenching belt of rain ahead of it.

After a while the rain was completely gone and the force of the wind subsided to a mere gentle breeze. Then the low grey and black clouds thinned and began to break up, so that the mid-morning sun was able to punch the warmth and brightness of its light out of the high, brilliantly blue infinity above.

This sunlight quickly warmed everything it touched and the breeze which was the final remnant of the storm retreated in the wake of the rain. Water droplets which clung to trees and rocks, meadow grass and earth, submitted to the abrupt change in the weather: and soon mist-like tendrils of steam started to show above the evergreen foliage of the pines. And this released a fresh smell of perfumed dampness that reached up the grassy slope to where the man stood in the doorway of the shack.

He breathed in deeply through his nostrils and squeezed his eyes tight closed, giving free rein to just one of his senses. But not for long. His ears picked up the first tentative sounds of birdsongs and he opened his eyes again and stepped out into the long, lush grass that grew right up to the warped and rotted walls of the shack. He looked in every direction across the mountainscape, to as far as distant ridges would allow: saw birds in flight and listened to their calls, all the time smelling the fragrance of the wet pines and grass as they dried in the sun. He even became strongly aware of the way the first warmth of the day caressed the flesh of his face and seemed to draw the damp chill of a whole night and half a morning out of the pores. And when he parted his lips to smile his pleasure of the experiences he derived from four senses, the fifth one seemed suddenly to begin to work for him. He could taste something. A subtle and elusive flavour that defied attempts at identification for long seconds. Until a beating of wings against the warming air caused him to swing his head around and he saw an eagle taking to graceful flight from a ledge high on the rock face which reared up two hundred feet away from the back of the shack.

'Freedom, chump!' he murmured to himself, rasping the words through clenched teeth as he curled his lips back even further to broaden the smile into one of pure delight. 'You got the taste of freedom!'

He threw back his head, his joy filled eyes following the upward spiral of the soaring eagle, his lips widening to a point where they were set to vent a gust of laughter. But abruptly he stifled the impulse, clamping his mouth closed and raking his eyes away from the bird toward a distant point above the pine forest. He had seen something there, on the periphery of his vision, which replaced happiness with suspicion, caused his eyes to lose their brightness and take on the look of hard, slightly sheened pebbles: flat and almost lifeless.

What he had seen, and what he gazed at now, was a puff of greyness more substantial than steam. Smoke. From a freshly lit fire set with damp kindling. Which caught and gave off more smoke to rise like a solid column high above the treetops before air currents snatched at it and claimed it as part of their invisible own.

The man eyed this indisputable sign of another human presence in the valley with suspicion because he was Adam Steele. A man who had good reason to relish freedom; and a whole lot of reasons to be wary of all who shared it with him.

The small cooking fire was about two miles to the south east and might or might not be directly on the route he would have to take through the pine trees. But having seen the smoke, he dismissed it and its meaning from his mind and his face adopted an impassive expression as he turned and re-entered the dank interior of the broken-down and long abandoned shack. His bedroll was already neatly furled and his saddle-bags were packed. The fire in the rusty but serviceable stove on which he had cooked supper last night and breakfast this morning was long dead. So it took him only a few seconds to gather up his gear and carry it outside, closing the door behind him to help preserve for future weather-ravaged travellers the minor comforts which the delapidated building offered.

His gelding waited patiently in a lean-to stable out back of the shack; well fed on the grass which grew inside and watered from the iron trough which was supplied by a downpipe with rain off the low pitched roof. The dappled grey horse continued to stand quietly as Steele saddled him and lashed the bedroll into place. But snickered and scraped at the ground as soon as he was led outside; energetically eager to be on the move.

'Easy, boy,' the man said to the animal, stroked the neck and swung up into the saddle, keeping a tight hold on the short rein. He touched his heels lightly to the flanks to command a slow walk. 'We've got a long way to go and all the time in the world to get there.'

Steele's voice held an accent that provided an unmistakable clue to his origins in the state of Virginia and perhaps, if he cared to think about it, that was the destination he had in mind when he spoke softly to the gelding. But, should he consider the matter more deeply, he would have to admit that if he was riding toward any place more specific than the next bend in the trail, it was somewhere that would remind him of Virginia. For he could never go back to reclaim his birth-right.

And this being so, he did in truth have all the time in the world to get where he was going. Would never arrive unless it proved to be that only in death did a man achieve all he desired in life.

Adam Steele had been born the son of one of Virginia's wealthiest plantation owners and throughout his formulative years had enjoyed all the privileges this entailed: seemed set as he grew out of youth into adulthood to become a replica of his father. A southern gentleman of the finest kind, using his wealth and position wisely and regarded with respect by all who came into contact with him.

A short lifetime of few but crowded years away from the unshaven, dishevelled and wary western drifter who now rode his horse down off the sloping meadow and into the aromatic pine forest of an Oregon valley. A man of below average height —he stood only a half inch above five feet six—but with a look of powerful strength in the way his one hundred and thirty pounds was stacked to his frame. A man in his late thirties who could appear to be several years younger on the infrequent occasions when he smiled but who mostly looked older because he had that kind of face. A face that once had been nondescriptly handsome and lacking in character: but which now seemed to tell conflicting facts about the man with every line and angle of its construction.

It was a lean face formed by regular features, with coal black eyes, a finely sculptured nose and a gentle mouthline. The long sideburns which he allowed to grow down a level below the lobes of his ears and the hair which he kept short on the back of his neck was prematurely grey, showing just here and there an odd strand of its former red. His skin was burnished to a nut brown by sun and wind and rain, furrowed by countless lines, reminiscent of old, uncared for leather. Anyone who glanced casually at the Virginian was inclined to be influenced by the basic structure of the man's features and the slightness of his build — more often than not judge Adam Steele to be a man out of his element. A small man, in more ways than one, who must have lost his sense of direction to find himself riding the big country. But those who had cause to take more than a first glance at him were quick to alter their opinion. If they had the perception to recognise that it was not merely exposure to the elements which had cut the lines in his face. Nor the passage of the years. Harsh experience of mental and physical suffering had inscribed many of the lines and deepened others. This same experience had also affected the man below the surface of the roughened and toughened skin, the very character of the man. This was more difficult to detect, unless he had cause to reveal it by his actions. For most of the time it was only hinted at by the way he moved, surveyed the world about himself with brief displays of emotion and responded with instant suspicion to something so innocous as a puff of wood fire smoke in the distance.

Short in stature he may have been, but it soon became apparent to anyone who spent more than a few moments in his company that Adam Steele was long on many other things. Experience of the more brutal facets of life, ability to foresee the signs of new evil and a capability to deal with it.

As he rode now through the towering trees, his lean face sheened with sweat in the humid atmosphere of sun after rain, he steered the gelding along the easiest course: first one way and then the other to by-pass clumps of brush. And his cold, flat, pebble-like eyes looked for danger while his ears strained to pick up sounds which might provide an earlier warning. He appeared to be riding in a relaxed attitude, sitting easy in the saddle and the reins held tightly in his hands simply because his mount was eager to make greater speed. In truth, his muscles were knotted so that his body and limbs were poised and ready to respond instantly and instinctively should his eyes or ears pick out a danger signal.

Although he veered the gelding to left and right, his overall route was to the south east: the mid-morning sun constantly visible directly ahead of him above the tops of the high growing pines.

Like the man who wore it, his clothing was also a mixture of two styles. An expensively tailored city suit of a pale blue colour, with a purple vest, lace trimmed white shirt and black bootlace necktie. The kind of outfit that a rich dandy might buy in New York, New Orleans or Richmond, Virginia. This one happened to have come from a high price store in San Francisco. The black riding boots which he wore under the cuffs of his suit pants were in keeping with his other fine clothing. Not so the grey silk kerchief which was hung loosely around his neck, the low crowned, wide brimmed black Stetson on his head and the black buckskin gloves which fitted his hands so tightly. These were strictly uncitified and had his fine clothing been in fine shape they would have struck harsh notes of contrast. But as it was on this late spring morning, every item of Steele's apparel was as worn and roughly used as the man himself. Torn here and there, stained by sweat, scuffed and dirty. And thus did it all merge into a composite whole without any hint of awkwardness.

So that a true city dandy might look at the man astride the gelding and frown in scornful criticism of the mode of dress. Whereas the average westerner would simply regard the Virginian as a dude who had made sensible compromises in order to ride the Oregon high country.

Steele smelled the smoke he had seen from the doorway of the shack and continued to ride and steer the horse in the same way as before. And made no effort to look for a convenient detour to left or right when he heard men's voices directly ahead of him: maybe three hundred feet away through the arrow straight trunks of the pines. Just two movements of his right hand showed that he was prepared for trouble should his resolute ride south east result in an encounter with the men who were yelling at each other. Three men. And a woman.

His right hand dropped away from the saddlehorn where his left continued to rest, holding the reins: went to a split in the outside seam of his right pants leg — the gloved fingers probing briefly through the gap to touch the wooden handle of a knife that jutted from a boot sheath. Then, having checked that the recently purchased knife was where it should be, he raised his hand again but only as far as his thigh to leave it lay there, three inches from where the fire scorched stock of a Colt Hartford revolving rifle protruded from the boot.

Rode in this attitude out from between two high growing clumps of brush and on to an area of swampy grass at the side of a narrow trail. The gelding vented a snicker of fear as he felt his hooves sink into the waterlogged ground. And made to rear.

'Oh my God, Johnnie!' a woman shrieked. 'It's a man!'

Steele needed to concentrate all his attention upon staying astride the panicked gelding and soothing the animal back to calmness. It took perhaps ten seconds to do this, during which time he received a fleeting impression of three Conestoga wagons stalled on the trail, three wearied four-horse teams and six people — three men and three women. Youngsters who had been struggling to free the lead wagon from the axle deep mud into which it had been dragged. Frightened youngsters all of a sudden: fearing the worst from the lone intruder who had ridden up to them without warning.

The rain water had not flooded the grassy bank so badly as the dirt trail and when the gelding responded to his rider and stood still, he sank no lower than up to his fetlocks.

Out on the trail, the three young men stood knee deep in thick mud. One of them was aiming an ancient Navy Model Colt at Steele and as the gelding became still the other two drew matching revolvers from their holsters and pointed the guns in the same direction. Despite the fact that they had the drop on the lone newcomer, the men looked as nervous as the three women who stared fearfully at the Virginian from under the forward jutting canvas cover of the bogged down Conestoga.

'Name's Steele,' the Virginian greeted evenly, not revealing by his voice or expression the self anger he felt for having ridden his horse on to marshy ground while he looked for a different brand of trouble that had probably never existed. 'I'd like for the grave to have a marker with that on it.'

'What?' This from the man who had drawn first. He had blond hair and was a head taller than the other two.

'If you're aiming to kill me,' Steele augmented.

'Shit, we don't want to do that, mister!' The youngest of the three. Probably no older than eighteen and trying to look older by cultivating a moustache.

'So put away the guns, why don't you?'

'In a friggin' pig's ear!' the tall, blond youngster snarled.

'No, kid,' Steele countered, his voice harsher. 'In the holsters.'

'Johnnie, do like he says,' one of the women urged anxiously. More girl than woman. All three of them were. Not yet twenty, any of them.

'Stay out of this, Sara!' Johnnie shot back, his tone harsher than before. 'We ain't takin' no chances, remember?'

Sara looked like somebody who has realised she made a mistake. The other two girls expressed the same brand of grim determination as Johnnie.

Steele nodded. 'A chance is sure what you kids are taking now.'

'On what?' Johnnie was contemptuous of a man making threats against three cocked Colts.

The Virginian raked his unblinking eyes from the point where the trio of men stood to the forelegs of the gelding and back again. 'Range of thirty feet. Personally I'd never trust a Navy Colt to be accurate over that distance. So you're taking a chance on having some luck. To put at least one bullet into me that'll kill me. You don't do that, you're not going to be able to move fast enough in that mud to get out of the way in time.'

'Aw, shit!' the kid with the moustache growled, and thrust his gun back into the holster. 'This is friggin' crazy!'

Johnnie shot a fast, angry, scowling glance at him. Then snapped his head around to glare at the other boy in the same manner as he heard:

'Phil's right, damnit!'

The second Colt was pushed clumsily into its holster. As Sara expressed relief and the other two girls shared Johnnie's disillusion about the actions of his companions. But the boy who still aimed his revolver was the most badly affected: looked mad enough to need an outlet for his rage.

Steele eased his left foot out of the stirrup, prepared to power off the saddle, draw the rifle and cock and fire it as he went toward the sopping wet grass. Provided Johnnie did not have the good luck to explode a lethal shot into him midway through his move.

The cooking fire was back down the trail, behind the last of three stalled wagons. As Johnnie made to look back at the Virginian after showing his feelings toward the other two young men, a log split with a sharp crack. And the tense Johnnie swung his Colt and gaze toward the sound.

'Watch out!' Sara screamed.

Phil and the other youngster made to draw, but fear served to add to their inexpert clumsiness. Johnnie was fast to correct his error. But not fast enough. Even before his arm had swung halfway around the arc to bring his Colt back to aim at Steele, the Virginian had powered upright in the stirrups, slid the rifle from the boot, thumbed back the hammer and squeezed the trigger. Steele fired from the hip, the Colt Hartford angled slightly down between the pricked ears of the gelding. The bullet impacted with the cylinder of the revolver, tearing it from Johnnie's grasp with enough force to bring a cry of pain from the youngster's gaping mouth.

The other two male members of the party snatched their hands away from the butts of their holstered Colts and stared in awe at the damaged gun as it sank into the mud. Johnnie shook his injured hand vigorously, then squeezed it under his left armpit, grimacing when these actions failed to ease the pain. The three girls gazed fearfully at Steele as the Virginian slid the rifle back into the boot and sat down in the saddle, taking up the reins in both hands.

'Gee, mister,' Phil said huskily and gulped. 'That just has to be the best damn shot I ever did see.'

'Or the friggin' luckiest!' the boy with the injured hand and the damaged pride growled.

'If there was any luck involved, John Carter!' Sara flung at him, 'then I'd say it was all yours! That this gentleman chose to shoot the gun from your hand instead of the pig head off your shoulders!'

Steele nodded to the auburn haired Sara as he heeled the gelding into movement and tugged on the reins to turn the animal toward the fiercely burning fire. 'Seems you've got a wise head on your shoulders, miss.'

'Mrs,' the girl replied quickly. 'We're all newly married.'

All three girls blushed when Sara revealed this fact. And for some reason expressed anxiety. Steele glanced away from them and across to where the trio of young men continued to stand in front of the team hitched to the bogged down wagon, up to their knees in mud: one of them grimacing his pain and the other two chewing on their lower lips, eyes filled with misery.

He showed his boyish grin that acted to drop several years away from his deeply lined face. And said wryly: 'Never does rain but it pours, does it?'

CHAPTER TWO

'HELP your friggin' self!' John Carter snarled after a short silence as all the youngsters watched Steele ride to the rear of the last wagon in line, swing down from his saddle, take a mug from his bedroll and lift the coffee pot off the fire.

'Reckon I'm owed it, kid,' the Virginian replied as he dropped down on to his haunches and sipped at the hot, strong drink, his gaze fixed upon the leaping flames. 'One cup of coffee for one bullet. Isn't it said that fair exchange is no robbery?'

'The hell with it!' Carter snarled. 'Come on, you guys. Let's get this friggin' wagon outta this shitty mud!'

They started to jerk on the harness and yell at the hapless draw team. Two of the girls aboard the Conestoga added their higher pitched voices to the din, but used more mild expletives. Steele was not aware that Sara had withdrawn from the struggle until she came to a halt on the far side of the fire from where he squatted. He came erect and touched a gloved hand to the brim of his hat.

'At first we thought you might be fixin' to rob us, Mr Steele. Or worse.'

She was eighteen or nineteen. Three inches shorter than Steele with a pale complexioned face in process of maturing from adolescent prettiness into the full-fledged beauty of womanhood. She had large green eyes surrounded by luxuriantly long lashes and a full mouth which looked like it might easily form into the shape of a sullen pout at the least opportunity. Her red hair was cut short, hugging the contours of her head without any curls. Her figure was slender, the curves of her high breasts and her hips seeming somehow more sensual because of their lack of fullness. Whether by accident or design, she was making the most of the sparseness of her body by wearing a snug fitting man's check shirt and a pair of equally revealing denim pants. Now that the danger of sudden death was passed, she exuded an almost haughty quality of self-assurance.

'Forget it, ma'am.' He dropped down on to his haunches again and resumed drinking the coffee.

'You saw the smoke from the fire, I guess?'

'Right.'

'You lookin' for somebody, Mr Steele?'

'No.'

'Just idle curiosity then?'

The Virginian pursed his lips and nodded toward the trees on one side of the trail. Then hooked a gloved thumb to indicate the timber which grew behind him. 'I was coming from there and heading in that direction, ma'am. It just so happened that you kids got yourselves bogged down between there and there. Soon as I've finished the coffee, I'll be on my way again.'

Sara pouted her mouth and the expression this formed detracted from her good looks: caused her to appear younger but far less attractive — like a spoilt child who has failed to get her own way. 'We could use some help, Mr Steele. Everythin' we try just seems to sink the wheels deeper in the mud.'

'Sara, damnit!' Carter yelled. 'Come on back here! We're gonna try unloadin' the friggin' wagon! These no-account nags ain't gonna haul it out the way it is!'

'He your husband, ma'am?' Steele asked.

She seemed reluctant to reply, then nodded, withdrawing her lips from the pout and compressing them into a thin line.

'He manage to speak clean while the preacher was conducting the wedding service?' Steele drank the last of the coffee and hurled away the wet grounds as he stood up.

'They're all like that. Phil Shelby and Al Yancy, too. Guess it makes them feel grown up. Will you help us? Some extra muscle could just do it, don't you think?'

Steele gestured with his hand toward the second and third wagons. 'What I think is that you kids should unhitch the other teams and have all the horses haul each of the . . .'

'That's it!' Sara Carter cut in excitedly. 'Why didn't we figure that out for ourselves?'

The Virginian showed another of his boyish grins as he unfastened the reins of the gelding from the rear wheel of the third Conestoga. 'If I was newly married to a young lady like you, I reckon I wouldn't be able to think too clearly, ma'am.'

Her pale cheeks flushed again, but she smiled her enjoyment of the flattery before she turned and ran along the sides of the wagons and teams to where the other two girls were climbing down to the trail. One of them was a match for Sara's height but with a fuller figure that verged on fatness. She had long blonde hair that cascaded to her shoulders in a mass of sun-glinting curls. The other was close to six feet tall and very thin. She was a blonde, too, but her hair was straight, tied with a black ribbon at the nape of her neck and then falling like a horse's tail to her waist. She had narrow hips and breasts that were small and pointed. The shorter girl had a face which suggested a cheerful nature and this gave her an innate attractiveness. The tall one's features were too angular and a bad, blotchy complexion was another cross she had to bear. Like Sara, both of them were dressed in Levi's and men's shirts.

'Hey, you guys!' Sara yelled. 'Ben Steele's come up with the answer! We should use all the horses on each wagon!'

Phil Shelby hit his forehead with the palm of a hand. 'Shit, why didn't we think of that first off?'

He was five and a half feet tall, with a broad, strong looking build. He had a head of tight curled black hair and a round, deeply bronzed face. With the kind of mouth that looked as if he smiled a lot and a quality in his blue eyes that suggested his brawn made up for a lack of brains.

'I did,' the six feet tall, slimly built, sullenly good looking John Carter rasped, glaring his continuing anger toward Steele as the Virginian swung smoothly astride the gelding. 'But it seemed like too much friggin' trouble to go to. Unload the Goddamn wagon, you women!'

'The hell with that, John!' Al Yancy retorted as he started to wade out of the patch of sucking mud, needing to hold on to the team's harness to haul himself along. 'Movin' horses around just has to be easier than takin' all the gear off the friggin' wagons and then puttin' all the shit back on again!'

Yancy was both short and skinny. Almost puny looking. He had a thin, pleasant face and wore wire framed spectacles with thick lenses which magnified his soft brown eyes. His hair was brown, too, neatly trimmed and slicked down to either side of a central parting. The denim pants, shirt and jacket he wore—an identical outfit to those of Carter and Shelby—seemed to be at least a size too large for his frame. When he spoke an obscenity, he always puckered his eyes which caused his cheeks to push up the spectacles.

'Frig it!' Carter roared. 'We agreed I was boss of this outfit, didn't we? What the hell's use of somebody bein' the Goddamn top man if you sonsofbitches don't do like I tell you?'

Shelby followed Yancy's lead and grunted with exertion as he struggled to get clear of the mud and up on to solid ground. As Steele urged his mount through the sopping wet grass.

'See what you done, mister?' the ill-tempered Carter snarled after his questions failed to draw a response from his wife and friends. 'Before you showed up we was gettin' along real fine!'

'Seems to me,' the Virginian answered as he steered the gelding around the area of mud and on to the trail beyond, 'that you weren't getting along at all.'

'Up your ass, shorty!'

'Johnnie!' Sara shrieked, suddenly afraid again.

But Steele neither said nor did anything in response to the abuse. Simply rode on down the trail and around a curve that carried him out of sight of the six youngsters and the three stalled Conestogas: slow and easy. But not in the same way he had approached through the pine forest, for his mind was now as untroubled as his attitude suggested and this attitude was not a pretence. There never really had been any inherent danger in the situation he had come upon and what happened had largely been as a result of his own suspicious nature. So how could he make the kids pay for the fast gun and bad mouth of one of their number? Especially since they had youth and inexperience on their side.

Once he had been like them, but for him and a few hundred thousand like him, a war had happened. A bloody, cruel, deadly war which only fanatics wanted and only fools enjoyed. But which ultimately proved a blessing in disguise for men such as Adam Steele. Men who were mere boys at the start but who had to grow up fast in order to survive. It could be argued, and the Virginian had once indulged in tacit discussions with himself, that if it had not been for the war, then he would not have become the kind of man he was now. But he had soon abandoned such futile lines of thought, since the clock could not be turned back. He was what he was and the events which had made him so were beyond reliving.

Sara Carter had made the same mistake as many others when she called him Ben Steele: had obviously, as she approached him at the fire, read the engraved gold plate screwed to the scarred rosewood stock of the Colt Hartford in the boot slung from the saddle of the hitched gelding. TO BENJAMIN P. STEELE, WITH GRATITUDE—ABRAHAM LINCOLN.

Ben had been his father, the man who had built up from nothing the Virginia plantation which had provided himself and his son with a fine living and which one day was due to be inherited by the younger Steele. But because of that bitter War Between The States, the Colt Hartford rifle with its engraved plate was all that Ben Steele was able to pass down to Adam.

The elder Steele died in a bar-room in the city of Washington on the same April night that Lincoln was assassinated: the President struck down by a bullet, his friend murdered by a lynch rope. It should have been a night of celebration for the Steele father and son, as they forged a reconciliation: putting behind them the bitterness which was caused while Ben worked as an agent for the Union intelligence in opposition to the Rebel Confederacy which numbered Adam as a cavalry lieutenant.

But Ben had died before Adam reached their pre-arranged meeting place—to cut down the corpse and fire his first shot in the violent peace which was destined to be, in many respects, more brutal than the war. That first shot killed one of those who conspired in the murder of his father. Many more had escaped from the city and when the newly mustered-out ex-trooper set off to track down and take his revenge against them, it was never his intention to become the kind of man he was now as he rode through a valley of Oregon's Blue Mountains.

He was simply a man trained to kill his enemies with one final battle to be fought before he assumed, earlier than expected, the role of plantation owner amid the green pastures and gentle hills of Virginia. But even before he fired the second shot of that battle, he discovered that he had lost his birthright as well as his father: that his home had been burned to the ground by southerners less ready to forgive and forget than Adam Steele. Of greater consequence than this though, in shaping his future life, was the fact that in tracking down and killing the lynchers of his father, he was faced with answering to the law for his actions — or killing one more man. A lawman. A deputy sheriff from Virginia who had been his boyhood friend.

Jim Bishop died. Not by the rifle which had ended the lives

of its previous owner's murderers. Instead, was throttled by an Oriental weapon of strangulation which Adam Steele had learned to use during his vengeance hunt—the thuggee's scarf which now hung loosely around his neck: looking like merely a kerchief unless it was noticed that two diagonally opposite corners were weighted.

The matter of whether or not Bish needed to be so cold-bloodedly killed was another line of futile thought which Steele had long ago abandoned. For in terms of the present the death of the young deputy-sheriff was of consequence only in as far as it had locked a door which was already firmly closed.

The Virginian stayed on the trail since it was easier to ride than the timber to either side and although it swung wide to left and right, it nevertheless took him in the direction he wanted to go—south east from one end of the broad valley to the other. He rode through the high pine trees for the rest of the day, the ground he was covering starting to rise as the sun turned red and began to slide behind the distant western ridges. At first the incline was gentle but it soon grew steeper and the trail had to veer sharply to either side, switching back on itself in a series of hairpin turns, in order that heavily laden wagons could be hauled up to the pass that was the only exit from this end of the valley.

By the time he emerged from the timber the sun was completely lost to sight and the bright half moon and a myriad of sharply glinting stars featured the cloudless night sky. As he followed the switchbacking trail which cut among rocks and gullies and clumps of hardy vegetation clinging tenaciously to sparse pockets of soil, the mountain air grew colder, biting at those areas of his face not protected by a two day growth of bristles. He dismounted, took a sheepskin coat from where it was lashed to his bedroll and shrugged into it, turning up the collar. Then he led the gelding by the reins over the final length of constantly turning trail to the rock-sided pass. Walking fast to combat the cold. At the high point, beyond which the terrain fell away in steps toward the Snake River glinting threadlike in the far distance, he made night camp and cooked a meal of jerked beef and beans on a brushwood fire.

Afterwards, while he sipped a cup of coffee, he washed and shaved for the first time in two days. And found himself regretting that he had purchased only three items in addition to the usual supplies when he was in San Francisco several weeks ago. He tried to block from his mind thoughts of why he should feel this regret tonight.

It had been a bad time in San Francisco, the latest of many troubled times on the aimless trail which had brought him from the place where he strangled Jim Bishop to this pass through a range of Oregon mountains. So many years and miles ago he had thought it necessary to kill his best friend in order to escape justice: only to discover that as a free man he drew a punishment more severe than the law could have devised. For as he drifted from one town to another, one river crossing to the next, riding plains and deserts and high country in every kind of weather all over the west, the threat of death was his constant companion. And to survive he had to be as ruthless as his enemies, using in the violent peace the war-taught skills he had been determined to forget when he rode into Washington that misty April night so long ago.

Many times he had tried to escape the destiny which his ruling fate had mapped out for him. To raise enough money and to find the ideal place where he could rebuild something akin to the fine life in Virginia he had always believed to be his by right. But on each occasion when such a dream seemed within reach, it was snatched violently away from him: until he was forced to acknowledge that all he would ever be allowed to keep was his life and his freedom. Those very things for which he had killed Bish. And he would have to keep on killing if he was to preserve them.

In San Francisco he had lost his freedom for a while, and once more had come close to losing his life: had escaped and survived with a stake of five thousand dollars and some bitter-sweet memories of a beautiful woman who was not all she seemed. He stayed in the city only long enough to buy a horse, a new knife to replace the one stolen from him, a warm coat which was identical to the one lost during an earlier life-and-death struggle and food for the trail.

Then he rode north for no good reason. Through northern California and up into Oregon. Swung north east and then south east. Riding around towns and buying fresh supplies as he needed them from isolated farmsteads and ranches. Paying a fair price for what he bought and never sparing time to stay and talk with the company starved farmers and ranchers and their families. In a hurry solely to get away from people: living rough and caring nothing for his appearance.

Which was a new departure for Adam Steele for, prior to his enforced stay in San Francisco, he had clung tenaciously to the last, pitifully few links with the life he used to enjoy. At every opportunity, he had purchased fine clothes, eaten good food in the best available restaurants and relished sleeping in the bed of a hotel room. While out on the open trail he had always washed-up and shaved and made the effort to keep his dudish clothing as clean as possible at the start and end of each day.

So what had happened to him in San Francisco that changed him? Not only his outward appearance, but also his attitudes—his very character.

'Renita,' he murmured, perhaps not even aware that he spoke the name of a Mexican whore: for his lips formed the word as the darkness of sleep closed in on his mind. A darkness much blacker than that of the Oregon night. Dreamless.

A distant sound roused him and he came awake instantly, his mind flooded with the light of total recall. His eyes cracked open and yet still appeared to be closed. His right hand instinctively tightened its grip around the frame of the Colt Hartford which lay alongside him beneath the blankets. His gloved thumb pressed against the hammer but did not pull it back. More sounds reached toward him through the moonlit darkness of late night and he opened his eyes fully and turned his head to search for their source as he identified them.

The clop of shod hooves, turning wheel rims and creaking wagon springs. He lifted his head from the pillow of his saddle and sat upright, the blankets falling away from his torso as he saw first the one and then the other two Conestogas make the final turn in the twisting trail and start up the last stretch of incline to the pass.

By the time the wagons came to a halt in a line between the high walls of rock which formed the pass, the Virginian had risen from his blankets, stirred up the grey ashes of the fire until they glowed red, added fresh brushwood and set a pot of coffee down in the flames.

'We can take care of our own needs, mister!' John Carter greeted ungraciously as he scowled down from the driving seat of the lead wagon. 'We might not even stopover here.'

His eyes were red-rimmed and had dark circles under them. Sara, who rode beside him, showed similar signs of weariness. But she had enough energy to fuel her anger.

'Then you go find another place and take care of yourself!' she snarled at her new husband. 'I'm too bushed to go any further tonight!' She flashed a smile toward Steele, who had returned to his blankets and sat down, using them to cover his legs and draping his sheepskin coat over his shoulders. 'I'm most grateful for your hospitality, Ben. I'm sure the others will be as happy to accept as me.'

'Damn right!' Phil Shelby called from the second wagon.

'Sure thing!' the bespectacled Al Yancy agreed.

These two boys climbed down from the seats and helped their wives off the wagons. Carter remained seated in sullen silence aboard his Conestoga while Sara sprang enthusiastically to the ground.

'It's not Ben, ma'am,' Steele said. 'Name's Adam Steele.'

She had gone to the rear of the wagon and was working on the tailgate fastenings. 'But on your gun it says . . .'

'Lincoln and my Pa were buddies, ma'am.'

'Oh, I'm sorry.'

'What you get for reading other people's rifle stocks,' he replied with a grin.

Shelby and Yancy, their pants legs caked with dried mud, made directly for the fire while their wives began to take the makings of a night camp from the wagons.

'You kids have been riding,' Steele told them as the two boys dropped to their haunches and extended their outstretched hands toward the flames.

'What?' Yancy asked, having to stifle a yawn.

'The teams are more beat than you are. Usual for a man to attend to the needs of his animal before himself.'

'Frig it, the short ass is tryin' to take over again!' Carter snarled.

'Hell, can't we even have a cup of coffee before we do that?' Shelby asked.

'Do whatever you like,' Steele answered, having to make an effort to keep from watching every move Sara made as she unloaded two bedrolls and cooking and eating utensils from the back of the wagon. 'Just telling you how things are usually done.'

'Do like Adam says,' Sara instructed. 'He seems like a man who knows what he's talkin' about.'

The two boys at the fire grimaced their dislike for the chore, but rose and moved to attend to their teams. While all the girls brought the necessary supplies and equipment to the fire and began to prepare a meal of stew and dumplings. They had been wearing long, warm coats but soon they took them off as the heat of the flames drew the chill out of their bodies. And Steele found it more difficult to avoid looking at Sara Carter. Abruptly recalled having spoken the name of another woman just as he went to sleep some four hours ago.

John Carter sat for a long time on the seat of the stalled wagon, watching the activity around him with obvious scorn and ill-temper. Until finally, mumbling curses to himself, he climbed down and unhitched his team, watered them from one of the barrels lashed to the side of the wagon and hobbled them on an area of grass shared by Steele's gelding and the other two teams. Shelby and Yancy had already broken open a bale of hay which was enough for all the animals.

'Satisfied, mister?' the tall, good-looking youngster growled as he joined the group at the fire and took the cup of coffee his wife thrust toward him.

'Horses are, kid. Was thinking of them.'

'Don't call me kid!' Carter snarled. 'It's that kinda friggin' attitude toward us we're gettin, away from!'

'Here, eat your damn supper, John!' the youngster's wife told him, pushed a plate into his free hand and ladled stew on to it. 'Maybe with your mouth filled with food you'll keep quiet for a while!'

'Don't you talk to me like that!' he retorted, swinging his angry glare toward her. 'We ain't friggin' married yet and even when we are I won't...'

He broke off, seeing the dismay which entered Sara's big green eyes. Then looked around at his companions at the fire and found them staring at him with a mixture of shock and anger. For a few silent moments he expressed anxious regret. Then stoked the fires of his own ill-humour as he shot a glance across to where the Virginian sat.

'Shit, what does he care about us not being hitched? And why the frig should we care what he thinks anyway?'

Sara flung the ladle down into the stewpot, got to her feet and advanced on Steele. She stood three feet away from him, her slender body silhouetted against the star pricked sky between the rock walls and the moonlight flattering her face to even greater loveliness.

'I think somebody should explain, Adam,' she said softly.

'I'm just sharing a night camp with you kids,' he answered. 'Your . . . Carter's right. None of my business what you share with each other.'

'Nothin'!' she came back quickly, heatedly. 'I'm Sara Yancy. Al's sister.' She waved a hand toward the tall, skinny girl with the long blonde hair and the morose expression. 'That's Gertrude Shelby, Phil's sister.'

'Call me Trudy,' the girl invited without enthusiasm.

'Shut up,' her brother snapped.

'And I'm Ron Carter,' the tubby blonde girl introduced with a cheerful smile that she quickly abandoned when she saw John glare at her. But added fast: 'Short for Veronica.'

Sara listened to the interruptions with impatience. Then continued: 'We're all from a small town named Shelterville up on the Columbia River. Don't suppose you've ever been there?'

'No, ma'am.' He clucked his tongue against the roof of his mouth, and corrected: 'Miss.'

'Call me Sara, please. It's a nice enough town I guess, but we . . .'

She broke off with a small cry of shock and raised a hand to clutch at her left cheek: to cover a tiny wound which suddenly appeared there, a droplet of blood expanding from the tear in the skin. Steele started his move before she began to raise her hand. Having seen the muzzle flash of a rifle above the rim of the pass's north rock face. Then heard the distinctive hiss of a bullet through air a split second before it hit a boulder two feet to his right. The crack of the rifle shot resounded between the walls of the pass simultaneously with the slap of the bullet's splinter-spraying impact.

It was one of these rock fragments that scaled upwards to bite into the girl's flesh. Then, before she could touch the source of the stinging pain she screamed louder: as Steele's shoulder crashed into her knees and sent her sprawling out on to her back.

Everyone in the pass knew what was happening by then, and yelled and shrieked their alarm as they hurled down cups and plates and scrambled for the cover offered by the big wagons. Then, reacting to the herd instinct, all of them converged on the central Conestoga: Trudy and Veronica huddling together in a joint embrace, the three boys drawing their Colts and swinging their gun arms to left and right—fear widened eyes searching for a target.

'Why did you . . . ?' Sara started as she made to get up. Then vented another cry of alarm as Steele stepped over her, caught hold of her right wrist and ran to the first wagon in the line, which was closest to him. The girl's shock turned to pain as she was dragged over the hard, rough ground.

'Get under there!' he barked at her, then released her wrist and straightened, flattening himself to the front wheel of the wagon as he saw another muzzle flash. In the same area as before.

This bullet dug up a divot of hard packed dirt from the centre of the trail.

'Oh, my God!' Sara moaned, and powered into a roll which carried her under the wagon. 'Somebody's shootin' at us!'

'Me, I reckon,' the Virginian rasped between clenched teeth. And lunged away from the wagon. Taking a sharp turn around the front of it and sprinting for the base of the cliff atop which the sniper was positioned.

'Where are you goin'?' Sara wailed in his wake, sounding like a frightened child, as a third bullet cracked from the rifle, hissed through the chill night air and burrowed into the dirt no more than a yard in back of the running Virginian.

He plunged into the deep moon shadow beneath the high rock wall and turned sharply left, in the direction that offered the greatest area of cover.

'Adam!' Sara shrieked, her tone rising and making her sound even younger.

'Quit it, you stupid bitch!' Carter flung at her. 'He ain't

got time to hold your friggin' hand right now! It's him that bastard on the cliff is shootin' at!'

Steele did spare the time—just part of a second—to reflect on the trace of jealousy that was mixed with the anxiety in Carter's voice.

'I knew he was trouble!' Trudy Shelby whined. 'I told you, didn't I tell 'em, Al? He's a gunslinger! We're all gonna get shot on account of him and . . .'

Flesh cracked against flesh and just before he lost sight of the central wagon Steele caught a glimpse of John Carter withdrawing a long arm after delivering the open-handed blow. Then heard the girl gasp and the boy rasp an obscenity.

'You didn't have to do that, Johnnie!' his sister complained.

The boy did not reply and his silence perhaps proved more effective than a whole string of curses would have been. For nobody else said anything either: all of them retreating into their own private worlds of fear and grievance.

Steele, although moving, probably made less noise than the six youngsters crouched under the wagons. For he breathed evenly, afraid but in control of his fear. Setting his booted feet down softly and taking care not to hit the rock with the Colt Hartford as he climbed steadily up a steep water course.

He had back-tracked to the valley end of the pass, having to stay tight to the cliff face for thirty or forty feet until he was beyond the point where the glow of the fire's flames made constantly moving inroads into the moon shadow. Then he moved out of the pass and began to climb, up the meandering gully which had been cut over millions of years by millions of tons of rain water and melted snow torrenting down from the high ground.

As he ascended the west facing slope he was in the full glow of the half moon: which was both a help and a danger. The light enabled him to see hand and foot holds and to spot where loose rocks and pebbles would rattle out from under him should he disturb them. But it also meant that he would be easily seen if the man with the rifle suspected an advance from this direction and silently changed his position to check.

But when the man did change his position he did not do it silently.

The Virginian was almost at the top of the fifty foot climb by then: less than five feet below where the water-made gully started at a point between two clumps of brush, the leafless branches of which resembled scores of emaciated fingers clawing hopelessly at the heavens. And there he halted, peering upwards, the Colt Hartford aimed at the empty sky between the brush. In a half crouch, balanced on the steep slope, rifle angled from his right hip and finger curled around the trigger. Listening to footfalls and a mumbling voice. Able to distinguish a few of the softly spoken words just before the man's head and shoulders showed between the dead branches.

'. . . got the sonofabitch. Iffen I hadn't done it don't make sense. Scared the hell outta 'em—Oh, Christ!'

He mumbled and moved like an old man, but he was one who could react fast when he thought his life was on the line. As he showed himself, not primarily interested in what was below him in the narrow gully, he was holding the Winchester in a two handed grip across his belly. But as soon as he caught a glimpse of the Virginian he swung the rifle and angled it downwards. Steele saw the hammer was back and had to assume there was a bullet in the breech.

'Hold it, I don't want . . .'

Steele spoke evenly, but knew the old man was not listening to the words. Would perhaps not have heard them if they had been shouted at him. He was too frightened. And too intent upon beating his fear by removing what frightened him.

The Colt Hartford cracked out a shot and the old man suddenly disappeared from between the two dead clumps of brush. Was hurled violently backwards by the bullet ripping into his chest: may even have been lifted bodily off his feet by the upward shot.

Steele did not see. For as soon as the Winchester slipped from the man's hands the Virginian squeezed his eyes tight shut. And did not open them again until the discarded rifle slid down the water smoothed gully and came to rest against his feet. Then he groaned a hardly audible curse and completed his climb to the top of the high rocky rise. Saw first the horse off to the left and guessed the man had been returning to the animal when he was frightened into the move which got him killed. The horse was hitched to a tree which was deformed by high winds, cropping contentedly at a patch of grass. The man lay spread-eagled on his back, death-glazed eyes staring up out of a time wrinkled face toward the infinity of the night sky. His hat, coat, pants and boots looked as old as he was. A large, dark, wet stain marked the front of the coat, left of centre.

'I don't know who you were, feller,' the Virginian murmured sorrowfully. 'So why did you make me kill you?'

The eyes remained fixed on the sky and the lips did not move out of their line which showed an expression of mild disappointment.

After Steele had unhitched the horse from the bent tree, led the animal to where the dead man lay and hefted the corpse up and over the saddle, a sour thought insinuated itself into his mind. He was alive, free and in possession of his father's gun. The old man's horse and gear were as serviceable as his own down in the pass. So why didn't he just swing astride the animal and ride? Away from whatever brand of trouble the kids were in. And, since he did not know the man who had tried to kill him, it was certain the oddly assorted bunch of youngsters were the reason for the attack.

But he dismissed the idea at once, and started to lead the horse by the bridle, following the sign which the old man had made on his ride to the top of the high ground. Which meant taking a long, circuitous route down to where the three boys and three girls were anxiously waiting.

Sara was under the central wagon with the others now and it was she who spotted Steele leading the corpse-carrying horse into the pass: and emerged first from the cover.

'What happened?' she called nervously.

'Somebody died,' he drawled without emotion.

The others came out from under the Conestoga. Al Yancy suddenly realised he was still gripping his revolver and he pushed it with hasty clumsiness back into the holster, as if ashamed to be caught holding the Colt.

'An old enemy?' John Carter asked, trying to sound hard and scornful but failing.

'A new one, kid.' He released the bridle and went to the fire, to squat down and pick up a cup half filled with now cold coffee. He emptied it and poured a fresh drink from the pot standing in the dying embers.

'Phil!' Trudy Shelby said as she took a step toward the horse with the body draped across the saddle. 'It looks like . . .' She lengthened her stride and then broke into a run over the fifteen feet gap. Came to an abrupt halt. 'Oh dear God in heaven! It is! He's killed Pa!'

The Shelby boy was in the centre of the group beside the wagon. But abruptly broke clear with an animalistic howl, his right hand clawing for the holstered Colt. But came to a sudden halt, frozen in the act of drawing: the rage in his eyes dying as he saw the Virginian's rifle aimed at him held one handed across the thighs of the squatting man. But that hand was fisted around the frame, a finger to the trigger and a thumb folding up from the hammer it had just cocked. Steele's other hand was wrapped around the cup, bringing it away from his lips.

'Often reckoned to be a praiseworthy ambition, kid,' he drawled, his soft spoken tone in total contrast to the harshness of his moonlit expression. 'But on this occasion I wouldn't like for you to follow in your father's footsteps.'

CHAPTER THREE

SARA YANCY lunged forward and halted between the boy and the man.

'No!' John Carter roared.

'Best give Johnnie or Al your gun, Phil,' the girl advised, her slender body tense with anxiety but her voice calm. 'Just until everyone's got over the shock.'

'He killed Pa!' Shelby said, having to force the words out around the lump in his throat.

Carter was standing immediately behind him and moved fast—to stretch out a hand and jerk the Colt from the distraught boy's holster. Shelby seemed totally unaware this had happened. When Sara stepped away, the son of the dead man stared at the Virginian but without rage now. There was a look of incomprehension in his dull blue eyes.

'Why?' he asked huskily, as his sister began to sob and fell to her knees, grasping a hand of her dead father.

'It was him or me, son,' the Virginian answered. 'Reckon you might be able to tell me why it was that way?'

Sara went to comfort the grieving girl. Veronica Carter seemed reluctant to do the same, more concerned with Phil's state of mind.

'Dearest,' she moaned.

'Get with the other women!' John snapped at his sister.

'Make some fresh coffee!' Sara countered, easing the weeping Trudy off the ground and forcing her to leave go of the dead man's hand. 'We need to talk. And be clear headed while we're doin' it!'

Steele pushed the Colt Hartford hammer to the rest and then left the rifle across his thighs as he wrapped both hands around the cup and sipped at the coffee. For what seemed a long time nobody said anything, while Veronica made a great deal of clumsy noise in setting a fresh pot of coffee to boil, putting wood on the fire and getting grounds and water from Shelby's wagon. Then emptying the cold dregs from the cups which had been left when the first rifle shot cracked through the night. Sara brought Trudy to sit down on the other side of the fire from where the Virginian squatted. The three boys moved over to the horse and carefully lifted down the corpse of the old man. Nobody looked at Steele.

'Guess nobody wants any more stew?' Veronica asked. And when nobody replied, added: 'No, I guess not'.

She hefted the cooking pot off the fire and carried it several yards away to spill its steaming contents on to the ground. Sara began to whisper soft words to Trudy Shelby. The boys talked quietly together where they stood beside the corpse which they had laid on the ground, legs together, hands clasped on the chest. Then, when Steele rose and started toward them, they moved as well. Grim-faced and still making a point of not looking at him as they angled to the side to avoid coming close to him on their way to join the girls at the fire.

But with his back to the youngsters, the Virginian sensed them watching him, suddenly silent again, until they realised he was ignoring the dead body and intended only to take care of the horse. He did this, taking the animal to hobble it among the others, removing the saddle and bedroll which he set down beside Phil Shelby's wagon. Then, after watering the horse, he went to sit down on his own saddle, again draping his sheepskin coat over his shoulders.

The voices of the youngsters at the fire reached his ears as a soft droning sound, rising and falling. Dull in tone for most of the time with just an occasional flare of challenge that was never accepted. Most of the talking done by Sara Yancy and John Carter.

'You hear anythin' of what we've been sayin', Adam?'

Steele looked up, his mind jerked out of a deep well of morose thought. Recognising the voice of the girl who had featured so prominently in his reflections. 'Got problems of my own,' he drawled, switching his impassive gaze between the girl, John Carter who stood beside her and the other four kids who were still sitting by the fire.

The Shelby brother and sister responded to his look with deep-seated bitterness. Carter was trying too hard to appear as unemotional as the Virginian. The rest gave the impression that a great weight had been lifted from their minds.

Despite the fact that he felt like a fool for doing it, Steele briefly searched the lovely face of Sara for a sign of something else beneath the surface expression she showed. But he found nothing.

'If you're talkin' about killin' Eric Shelby, we don't hold that against you.' She glanced over her shoulder. 'At least, most of us don't. After a while, Phil and Trudy'll feel the same as the rest of us, I guess.'

'You want me to say I'm grateful?'

'Of course not!'

'But you want something from me, I reckon?'

'Some of us do.' Carter put in irritably. 'Votin' was three against three.'

'Who was elected what, kid?'

'Don't call me . . . !'

'For God's sake, John!' Sara snapped. 'Stop actin' the big I-am! You didn't look so great when old man Shelby started firin' at us.'

The taunt expanded Carter's anger. Steele defused it by drawling: 'He did all right.'

The boy was surprised by the compliment. And Sara took advantage of the tension-easing silence.

'Look, Adam. We'll level with you. We're all of us runnin' away from home. There isn't one of us of age yet, so it was bound to raise cain back in Shelterville when our folks found out we'd gone.'

'They rather have you dead than playing house together?' Steele asked.

Her cheeks flushed in the moonlight. But with anger rather than embarrassment. She controlled her emotions, though. 'It's up to you whether you believe it or not. But like I told you before, there's nothin' like that goin' on. And we're all damn proud of that, comin' from a place like Shelterville. Because in that town folks are so downright strait-laced and prissy it just asks for the kids to kick over the traces.'

'Get to the friggin' point, woman!' Carter growled.

'Let me finish!' she threw at him and then moderated her tone. 'You have to know all of it, Adam, or the point won't make any sense to you.'

'Will it take long?' Steele asked. 'Be dawn in a couple of hours and . . .'

'Not long. Please listen?' She got an imploring look in her big eyes, but now the Virginian was able to prevent himself from reading something in the expression that might never be there. 'Shelterville is named for the Shelby and Carter families. Eric Shelby and Doug Carter got together the wagon train back in the 'fifties and led it from Independence, Missouri, and out on to the Oregon Trail. My own parents were on the train and there were thirty other families or couples along. These are three of the very wagons they travelled on.'

'They're like me,' Steele muttered, raking his eyes over the line of ancient Conestogas which showed many signs of the passage of time.

'What?' the girl asked, confused as her flow was interrupted.

'Showing their age.'

'You said it, mister,' Carter rasped.

Sara treated both of them to a glare of irritation. Then hurried on: 'Those people built the town up from nothin'. Raised crops and cattle and horses and set up stores to supply their needs. And everythin' went well for them. Too well for the young people like us, the way things turned out.'

Carter had started to be bored by the girl's story. Wore the expression of someone who had heard it all before, many times. He saw that Al Yancy was rolling a cigarette and making a hash of it. And accepted this as an excuse to return to the fire.

'One of the couples that were there at the beginning was a preacher and his wife. The Reverend Turner and Beth Turner and it appears the preacher had a powerful influence over the other folks. Any time anythin' looked like it was goin' wrong, he'd say a prayer and everythin'd turn out right.

'Now they weren't very bright people, our parents, Adam. Dirt farmers and store clerks and stock breeders in a small way. And it was easy for them to believe that all the luck they had was heaven sent on account of the Reverend Turner's prayin'. And so they started in to prayin' most of the time they weren't workin' or sleepin'. And I guess in those early days there wasn't any time left over for anythin' else.'

'You saying the whole town got religion, miss?'

She nodded vigorously. 'That's just it. Please call me Sara, won't you?'

'Sure thing.'

'Well, they got religion. Real bad. Or real good, maybe. Anyway, kinda like those Mormons in Utah. You heard of them?'

'I've heard of them.'

'Well, our folks didn't start nothin' new in the religion line,' she continued, as all three boys lit cigarettes rolled by Carter. 'But they sure as hell must be the strictest Episcopalians in all creation.' She grimaced at vivid recollections of living in Shelterville. Then sighed to end the pause. 'Anyway, it's a lousy place to live when a person's idea of a good time goes further than singin' hymns three hours every Sunday.' She shook her head. 'Well, not quite that, but you know what I mean?'

'I reckon.'

'That's fine. But you don't really, I guess. Nobody with a

mind of his own who ain't lived in a place like that can really understand what hell it is.'

'I'm old like the wagons, Sara,' he told her. 'But I've got some memories of what it was like to be young.'

'I guess so,' she allowed absently, then stared directly down into his half smiling face and spoke in a rush. 'Anyway, us six decided we couldn't take it no more. And not only because we wanted to get married and they got a strict rule in Shelterville that people must be twenty-five before they can do that. There just ain't one single, solitary thing about Shelterville we could take any more. So we upped and left. Took the wagons that belonged to our fathers, supplies from the larders of our own folks' kitchens and got out of that place. And we're gonna keep on goin' until our supplies run out when we're gonna work to earn money to buy more and then move on again. All they way to New York City. Where folks are free to have fun the way they want. Can you blame us for wantin' to do that, Adam?'

'Reckon not.'

'Will you help us?'

He nodded in the direction of the corpse. 'Why? You afraid your Pa and the Carter kids' old man will be as mad as he was, Sara?'

'Of course not!' she blurted, and shuddered. 'You should know about Mr Shelby. He was a widower. His wife died only last year and since then he's been a little . . .' She let the sentence hang, unfinished, and shot an anxious glance toward the fire.

'Father was a little cranky after mother died,' Trudy Shelby supplied dully.

'He was friggin' out and out crazy!' her brother snapped, glaring his enmity at Steele. 'But that was no reason to kill the poor bastard!'

Sara whirled angrily to face the whole group. 'For Christ's sake!' she shrieked. 'Are you gonna leave this to me or not?

If you ain't I'm gonna . . . gonna . . . Oh, damn, I don't know what I'll do!'

She sobbed once and sitting behind her, looking up at her, Steele saw her body and limbs become rigid as she struggled to control herself. But she failed and another sob wracked her. Then she covered her face with her hands and lunged into a run: racing across to the rear of the lead wagon. She climbed up into it.

Carter hurled his cigarette into the fire and made to rise.

'Leave her, John,' Al Yancy instructed sharply, his tone and expression contrasting with his former ineffectualness. 'You know what Sis is like when she gets into that kinda mood. She'll only get mad at you.'

Then he got to his feet and advanced on Steele, halted midway between the fire and the Virginian. 'We sure are actin' like a bunch of wet-behind-the-ears kids, ain't we, mister?' he posed, his face working so that his spectacles kept rising and falling, even though he was not cursing now.

'You really want me to answer that, son?' Steele asked him.

'Hell, no. I'll just finish tellin' you what Sara was sayin'. We've run out on a set-up where we don't agree with none of the rules. And it's likely my Pa and Mr Carter will come after us. Maybe the Reverend Turner and some others. They won't shoot at us the way Phil and Trudy's Pa did, but they'll sure as hell try to make us go back. And it ain't only that that worries us.' He glanced around him, at the area of the rock sided pass lit by the flickering flames of the fire and to the vast country which stretched away to either side, dark and ominous in the dead hours of the night before dawn. 'We're town people. Born and bred in Shelterville. Furtherest we've ever been before is to Portland. Only time we ever got out into the country was Fourth of July church picnics in a wood on the Columbia five miles north of Shelterville. Mister, you saw what kinda hash we was makin' when we got the wagon bogged down in the mud back there. And how we all hid under a wagon when the shootin' started.'

'That don't count!' John Carter growled, but then lowered his voice and evened his tone. 'It seemed right from the start that it was you bein' shot at. Which made it your trouble. And seein' as how it was Mr Shelby doin' the shootin', it figures he was out to get you. Must have got the idea into his crazy head that you . . .'

'Aw, quit it, John!' Yancy groaned. 'If Shelby aimed to kill Mr Steele, it was because he thought he was tied in with us. Which made trouble for all of us.'

He worked his spectacles up and down and his magnified eyes gazed at the Virginian, asking a tacit question.

'New York is about the last place in the world I reckon to go to, son.'

'As far as you are goin' then? Hell, we ain't so struck on New York, I guess. It's just that back in Shelterville it seemed like New York was the most number of miles away. We'll go any place you're headed.'

'So long as it ain't back toward home,' Veronica Carter added sourly.

'What for?' Steele asked as all five of them looked at him with eager expectancy. And he could sense Sara Yancy sitting tensely and listening hard to the exchanges while she hid in the Conestoga: perhaps having guessed that her brother's words had convinced the dissenters to go along with her idea.

'Because we don't figure we can make it on our own!' Yancy blurted.

Steele shook his head. 'Didn't mean that, son. Was asking about me.'

They all looked puzzled.

'He means why should he help us,' Sara called from the wagon. 'And what is he goin' to get out of it, I guess?' Her tone added the query.

Surprise, then disappointment took command of the youngsters' faces. And as the silence lengthened, the Virginian decided he was learning something more about this bunch of unlikely rebels against parental control. They may have been subjected to stern disciplines back home in Shelterville, but they were all badly spoiled: that within the confines of the firm religious rules, the kids were over-indulged and given everything they wanted without the need to earn it. So their first experience of an outside world in which nothing was for nothing came as a rude shock to them.

'We got no money to spare, mister,' Carter said to end the silence. 'Found is all we can offer.'

'And no arguments,' Sara added as she climbed out of the rear of the wagon. 'Everyone'll do exactly what you tell them.'

Steele slid down off the saddle and arranged his blankets and coat over him. As always, the Colt Hartford shared his bedroll.

'I'll sleep on it,' he allowed as he tipped his hat over his face, blotting out the fire and moonlight. But unable to keep from his mind a vivid memory of how the shirt and pants of Sara Yancy clung so snugly to her thighs and breasts as she clambered lithely down from the wagon tailgate.

'What about Pa?' Trudy Shelby asked morosely.

'Forget about that!' Sara answered curtly. 'The way it happened, it couldn't be helped and if we're gonna keep on . . .'

'I mean what about Pa's remains?' the other girl interrupted. 'We can't just leave the body layin' there like that. We gotta get him buried and say some words over the grave.'

'Well, we sure know enough prayers,' John Carter growled.

'But first you have to dig a hole,' Steele contributed from under his hat. 'And that's something you do yourselves. I'm having nothing to do with that kind of undertaking.'

CHAPTER FOUR

STEELE never expanded on those few sourly drawled words to accept the proposition the kids put to him, but by shortly after sunrise the next morning his actions made it quite clear that he would do as they asked. He was the first to awake at the camp, as the leading arc of the sun lanced a bright shaft of yellow light between the high rock walls of the pass.

As he rose from his bedroll, stretching the stiffness of sleep out of his muscles, he looked at the youngsters and saw that they were firmly segregated: the three girls sleeping quietly under the last wagon in line and the boys snoring beneath the first one. He was unable to tell which girl was which beneath the humps of their blankets and he called himself a fool for trying: kept busy to keep himself from trying again.

First he stirred redness into the embers of the dying fire, added fresh fuel and set coffee to boiling and washing and shaving water to heating. While he waited for the steam to rise and the aromatic fragrance of coffee to permeate the fresh, chill morning air of the mountains, he watered the horses and then moved over to where a mound of fresh earth showed at the foot of one of the rock faces. The grave was marked with a cross formed by two branches of brushwood tied together. The longer length had been pushed twice through a piece of cardboard that would not survive for many days in the sun, the wind and the rain of Oregon's high country spring climate. Crudely lettered in charcoal on the cardboard was the simple legend: ERIC P. SHELBY, DIED NEAR HERE. R.I.P.

When Steele had buried his own father back in Virginia he had not marked the grave. For people filled with hatred rather than the unprejudiced vagaries of the weather would have destroyed it: may even have desecrated the grave.

The kids slumbered in the sleep of the exhausted and came

awake with ill-humoured groans and growling complaints when the Virginian clanged the ladle against the cooking pot. He had washed up and shaved by then and was sitting by the fire drinking his first cup of coffee of the day.

'What friggin' time is it?' Phil Shelby snarled.

'We don't use clocks out in this kind of country, son,' Steele answered. 'There's just getting up time and bedding down time and in between there are eating times.'

'I'll fix breakfast,' Sara said eagerly.

'Do that,' the Virginian responded tersely: over-reacting to the warmth of arousal he felt in the pit of his stomach as he saw that, tousled with the effects of sleep, she was more desirable than ever. 'And you boys get the teams hitched to the wagons.'

'Hell. I ain't no use to nobody until after I've eaten in the mornin's,' Carter groaned.

'John, we said no arguments,' Sara warned.

'All right, all right!'

The boys did as they were told and while Sara fried bacon and grits the other two girls stowed the bedrolls in the wagons. The chores were done in truculent silence, except by Sara who hummed cheerfully to herself while she attended to the meal. Then, as they all ate breakfast, feeling the rays of the early sun take the chill off the mountain air, their moods improved.

'Where exactly are you headed, sir?' Al Yancy asked.

Steele showed that his disposition had not altered at all since he had forced himself to shield his feelings for Sara from her and the others. 'Another lesson for you, kid,' he answered coldly. 'Like there being no use for clocks out here. If you meet up with somebody who doesn't volunteer what his business is, you don't ask.'

The harshness of the man's response acted to dampen the newly risen spirits of the youngster.

'I'm sorry,' Yancy muttered.

'Chances are you'll be that a lot more times before we part

company, kid. I'll know the same as all of you will know whenever it happens. So there won't be any need for you to say it.'

He had used his own eating and drinking utensils and now he rose and cleaned them up himself before he packed all his gear and saddled the grey gelding.

'Is it all right if we wash ourselves and brush our teeth before we pull out, mister?' Phil Shelby asked with a disgruntled grimace.

'Good habits are best kept,' Steele replied and moved to check over the wagons, the teams and the way the horses had been put in their traces.

Although the Conestogas showed many obvious signs of their age and the gruelling journey they had made more than twenty years earlier, they were in a remarkably fine state of preservation. Rotted and warped timber had been replaced, the tarp covers were expertly patched and the axles and the wheel hubs were well greased. Inside each of them there was a large trunk, some cartons of supplies, a heap of blankets and a range of cooking and eating equipment. The lead wagon carried a dozen or so bales of hay. The water barrels lashed to the sides of all three had obviously been kept topped up whenever a stream or pool offered the opportunity for replenishment.

The horses were strong, healthy animals and had been hitched with expert care.

'They're Suffolk Punches,' John Carter said as he waited for Sara to pack away the last of the paraphernalia of the night camp. 'Bred from stock that came from England. My Pa raises all the horseflesh in Shelterville. And they're hitched right.'

The other two couples were already aboard their wagons. Sara called that she was all done.

'The Conestogas are in fine shape, too,' Steele said as he moved away to mount the gelding and Carter climbed up on to the driving seat of the lead wagon.

'Shelterville people don't waste anythin',' he answered. 'Reason they're all so rich, I guess.'

'Works out that way sometimes,' the Virginian drawled, reaching down to catch the reins of the dead Shelby's horse and leading the animal to the rear of the Carter wagon, where he hitched him to the tailgate. 'Let's go.'

He rode out ahead of the line of lumbering Conestogas, hat brim pulled low against the glare of the hot sun and squinting his eyes to peer into the distance. Out over the Blue Mountains foothills which were liberally sprinkled with stands of timber and cut with many water courses that all ran toward the broader strip of twisting and turning river that was the Snake. He could see the trail for perhaps a mile and a half as it swung to left and right, but always leading ultimately in a south-eastern direction. Not a part of the Oregon Trail because it was too far south for that. But an old trail, little used. Not a stage route. Probably an ancient army road established to supply isolated forts. Which meant that, for as long as it lasted out, the trail would be wide enough to take the wagons and could follow a course on up and down grades that would not put too much strain on the teams.

As the day progressed, the climbing sun grew hotter. There was nothing to suggest that the violent rain storm which lashed at the mountains the day before had spread this far east. For the ground was as dry as old bones. But more brittle, the parched upper crust crumbling beneath shod hooves and iron wheel rims: to rise as powdery dust that clung to sweat sheened flesh and irritated the sensitive membranes in the throats and nostrils of the three couples riding the wagons. Since he was out at the head of the slow moving column, Steele was less affected by this discomfort: had only to contend with the familiar unpleasantness of sweat which caused his clothing to chafe his skin, and muscle ache from sitting upright astride the gelding.

And he endured these minor irritations gladly, feeling again the something close to exhilaration he had experienced after the rain yesterday when he acknowledged to a seemingly empty world his relish of freedom. The kind of freedom he had taken for granted ever since he emerged from that terrible period of drunken remorse after the death of Jim Bishop: had never spared a thought for until he was made a prisoner by a fanatical group of would-be assassins in San Francisco. People who desperately wanted to kill a man but lacked the skill to commit the act: who literally seized upon Adam Steele because he was an expert marksman, in the full knowledge that although he might hire out his skill, he would never simply kill a man for money.

Renita had been a part of their plan to force him into making that killing shot. Renita, who was the first woman he had taken in a very long time: allowed him to use her body as a vital factor in the betrayal that led to yet another experience with evil and violence in the life of Adam Steele. As the name of the Mexican woman came into his mind again—this time while he was wide awake—he tried to visualise the way she had looked. But he could not and he felt no sense of loss because of this. She was the first person in a very long time, man or woman, who had meant something to him. And despite her lies and deceit which took advantage of his regard for her he had mourned her death. Without, perhaps, being consciously aware that this was the reason for his depression as he made preparations to leave San Francisco and then rode the many trails that brought him to the shack where he sheltered from the Blue Mountains rain storm.

'Hey, mister!' John Carter called. 'Ain't it about friggin' time we stopped to eat somethin' else besides this Goddamn dust?'

Steele did not turn to look back at the lumbering wagons. 'Half a mile further, kid,' he answered. 'Be some shade for us and the horses in that defile ahead.'

The trail did not enter the narrow gap between two mesalike rock formations, but curved to pass close by it and the Virginian had been paying particular attention to the area of shadow against sun bleached cliff faces ever since he was near enough to see it through the early afternoon heat haze. Not only because it seemed to offer the ideal place to stop: also because it provided good cover for anyone with evil intent to watch the trail. The only convenient point for an ambush since the short wagon train had pulled out of the pass.

And he continued to watch the entrance to the defile over every yard as he closed in on it. With no clearly definable reason for suspecting there might be trouble waiting there. On his guard because that was his way. It was also his way, he acknowledged to himself with a wry grin that nobody saw, to allow his guard to drop whenever a pretty woman caught his fancy. More especially if the pretty woman showed more than a passing interest in him. Even if the woman was little more than a girl, almost young enough to be his daughter.

He held up his hand and reined in his gelding to come to a halt some twenty feet short of the gap between the rocks. Not grinning now. Peering intently into the deep shade as he waited for the wagons to come to a standstill. Silence descended, heavy in the hot air.

'Well, what the friggin' hell are we waitin' for?' John Carter snarled. 'I'm Goddamn starvin'!'

'Hush!' Sara rasped. 'Adam's . . .'

'You'll live kid!' Steele drawled. 'Maybe.'

Metal scraped against metal and all six youngsters gasped and stared fearfully toward the defile, knowing the sounds came from somewhere within the deep shade between the rock walls. Perhaps identifying them. Or maybe unable to think clearly enough as panic gripped their minds.

The Virginian knew what the sounds were. The actions of repeater rifles as the levers were pushed down and forward and then snapped back.

'Smart man, wagonmaster,' a man said levelly. 'Everyone follows your example, they'll all get to live.'

It had not been possible to tell how many rifles had been pumped. And the crunch of slow moving footfalls on hard packed ground was also confusing, for the sounds bounced between the cliff faces.

'Need some eats is all. We're a lot hungrier than you people, I'd say.'

Steele's eyes adjusted to the darkness within the defile and saw the four men like moving shadows as they advanced on him, their rifles aimed from the hip. Men with filthy, unshaven faces. Bare chested. Wearing the uniform hats and pants of the US Cavalry. Three of them dragging their feet and weaving from side to side, sometimes bumping into each other. These three staring fixedly out of their sunken, glazed eyes at the Virginian as if he, sitting easily astride the gelding, were the only stable object in a constantly moving world.

The fourth man was at the end of the approaching line, to the right of where Steele waited. Taller and much younger than the others. As dirty and dishevelled as they were. But not so drunk. Perhaps not drunk at all.

'Stop here, you guys,' he instructed as all of them reached the end of the defile, still in the shade but clearly visible to the frightened youngsters and coldly afraid Steele.

The drunken men—all of them in their late fifties—obeyed the order as if they were automatons and the switch which controlled them had been thrown. But they swayed and had to shift their feet apart to remain upright. Their eyes continued to stare fixedly at Steele. Their rifle barrels dipped and rose, swung to left and right, as if to the dictates of a veering wind.

'You people got food, ain't you?' the thirty-some year old man asked, having raked his unglazed eyes over the line of wagons and now concentrating upon the Virginian.

'Put up the rifles and you'll be welcome to eat with us,' Steele said.

'Hell, let's just kill 'em and take, lieutenant!' the man at the other end of the line slurred.

He made the effort to control the swaying of his body and bring his Winchester to a steady aim.

'No, Brant!' the officer barked and snapped his head around to look along the line of men.

The Winchester cracked a shot that was shockingly loud as the report echoed between the high walls of rock. Too fast for Steele to take any evasive action, so that he survived simply because Brant was unable to place the shot accurately: the movement of the man's finger against the trigger causing the rifle barrel to dip just before the bullet exploded from the muzzle. Go low enough to miss the man but tunnel into the broad chest of the gelding.

'Adam!' Sara screamed, her voice piercingly shrill. 'Oh, no!'

The gelding snorted and dropped hard on to his front knees, the impact causing a great gout of liquid crimson to gush from the hole in its flesh.

Steele had snatched his feet out of the stirrups by then, one hand going to grip the saddlehorn as the other jerked the Colt Hartford from the boot: a gloved thumb clicking back the hammer as the forefinger hooked to the trigger. But he had no time or opportunity to squeeze off a shot. For the forward slope of the dying horse's back and then the roll of the animal on to its side acted to spill him painfully to the ground without a hope of controlling the direction he took or the attitude of his body and limbs. His head hit first, then his left shoulder. His side came down and trapped his elbow between hip and rock hard dirt.

With a groan of pain rasping between his clenched teeth, he pushed with the rifle and his legs to roll to the side: more afraid for those first few moments of the crushing weight of the doomed horse than of a rifle shot tearing into his body.

The ground vibrated as the horse carcase hit and became inert. Steele felt a sticky wetness on his face, shook his head to clear the blurring tears of pain from his eyes and looked up and away from the pool of horse blood into which he had pitched. Saw the line of four bare-chested men staring down at him: three with horror and one with an expression akin to ecstasy.

Stretched seconds drained away in the hot, dry silence of the Oregon afternoon. While Steele forced himself to recover from the paralysing effect of his fall and to quell the anger that had expanded to the dangerous proportions of a mindless rage. And the three men with unfired rifles in their hands swung their heads to gaze at the one who squeezed the trigger.

'You murderin' friggin' bastards!'

Not until the last of the screamed words had exploded into the stillness did Steele identify the voice of Sara Yancy. By which time the four men with rifles had all snapped their heads around to stare at the wagon on which she had been sitting. Was now standing, Carter's Colt in a double handed grip.

The revolver bucked in her hand, its bullet cracking high and wide of the men to blast chips of rock from the cliff face within the defile.

'That's my girl!' Steele murmured as his willpower won out over the debilitating effects of pain and he thrust forward the rifle and squeezed the trigger.

His shot took Brant in the centre of the chest and hurled the man backwards, the rifle flying from his grasp as his hands went to the blood oozing wound.

'Oh, Jesus!' Carter shrieked and snatched the revolver from Sara's two handed grip while she stared down at the gun, not comprehending why it failed to fire again when she squeezed the trigger.

'Don't kill us!' the lieutenant begged, and threw down his Winchester just as the muzzle of the Colt Hartford swung toward him. 'We ain't got no . . .'

Three gunshots sounded and the man was hit by a bullet that

drove deep into his belly. He went down on to his rump, legs splayed and expressing total hopelessness.

'. . . ammo,' he managed to force out as Steele raked the barrel of the rifle away from him to pick a new target.

But Steele did not fire, for both the other men had followed the younger one's example and thrown down their Winchesters. Even had time to emphasise their surrender by thrusting their hands into the air.

'Hold it!' he yelled, pushing himself up on to his knees and swinging his eyes toward the wagons. Was in time to see Carter, Shelby and Yancy leap down to the ground and fire their Colts as they started to run. Sprinting across the ground that gave up puffs of arid dust from beneath their pumping feet.

All three bullets went wide, one of them snagging into the unfeeling corpse of Brant.

'Sonofabitch!' Shelby yelled in high excitement and fired again.

This shot tore into the side of one of the older men as both of them whirled to start to retreat into the defile. He staggered for two running steps, then was hit by bullets from the guns of Carter and Yancy—one in the back of the head and the other in the thigh.

All three kids vented whoops of delight as they saw the blood pouring man pitch to the ground, a corpse before he hit it.

'Hold your damn fire!' Steele roared, jerking to his feet, and bringing up his rifle: intent upon sending a warning shot cracking across the narrowing gap between the fast running boys and the mouth of the defile where two men lay sprawled in death and one sat with an ugly hole in his belly and an expression of hatred on his face. But then he had to bring the Colt Hartford hard down to the ground, to prevent himself from toppling as the weakening effects of his fall off the dying horse robbed his legs of the strength to support him unaided.

The three revolvers cracked out more shots as the boys

skidded to a halt: six feet from where the lieutenant sat and flinched but did not duck as the bullets whined over his head to drill into the back of the running man. They found their aim because this time Carter, Shelby and Yancy took the time to line by their sights on the target: making bars of their left forearms and resting the gun barrels on them.

'We got him! We got the friggin' bastard! Let's finish off the sonofabitch!'

The lieutenant was not afraid to die. He looked up at the muzzles of the three Colts which were angled down at him and sneered his contempt and hatred toward the excited faces of the youngsters who were pointing the guns.

Steele ceased to use the Colt Hartford for a crutch, and staggered back two steps, swaying, as he splayed his feet wide apart and tried to bring the rifle to the aim. But then did not trust himself to be any more accurate than the man named Brant. Knew he ran the risk of shooting one of the boys or even the wounded lieutenant if he tried to fire between them. So he angled the barrel up at the infinity of the sky and triggered the bullet harmlessly toward the sun.

'I said to hold your damn fire!' he roared as all three boys snapped their heads around to stare back over their shoulders, startled by the unexpected crack of the rifle. Then were startled even more by the glare of depthless rage that the Virginian directed at them: the expression made to look even wilder by the horse blood that was smeared across his forehead and cheeks.

'Why the frig should we?' Carter demanded. 'All these cruddy bastards deserve to get it!'

'Oh, Jesus!' Al Yancy moaned as the last remnants of his excitement drained out of him and he raked his lens-magnified eyes over the crumpled, blood-run bodies. 'I'm gonna throw up!'

He did, spewing a great arc of vomit out in front of him. The sick had a greater effect on the wounded lieutenant than the threat of the guns a few moments ago. And with a yell of revulsion he ignored the agony of his belly wound and forced himself into a roll, out from under the spray of foul smelling substance which gushed from the boy's mouth.

Then Carter and Shelby side-stepped, retreating from where Yancy went down on to his haunches and then tipped forward on to all fours, still retching but unable to bring up anything more from his sucked-in stomach.

'All right, kid,' Steele allowed, getting both his voice and his expression under control. 'You still feel that way, kill him.'

Despite the pain and the prospect of a great deal more which menaced him if he should survive the single wound, the lieutenant abruptly discovered that life was sweet. And he stared in horrified disbelief at the man who had spoken the words—watching him with wide and unblinking eyes as the Virginian lowered himself tentatively to the ground, grimacing as the act of bending his legs and sitting down drew protests from the bruises of the fall.

'What?' Carter croaked, finally able to tear his disgusted gaze away from where Yancy was folded over, still retching drily.

'I said to kill him if you have to,' Steele answered, resting the stock plate of the rifle on the ground and turning the cylinder to eject two spent cartridge cases.

For a stretched second he thought he had misjudged the boy. For the disgust dropped from his face as he realised he was being challenged. And determination glinted in his dark eyes as he made to whirl his face and gun toward the helpless lieutenant.

'You can't,' the wounded man said, his voice no more than a whisper as he gazed up at Carter, squinting his eyes and probably seeing the boy as no more than a dark silhouette against the dazzling blueness of the sun bright sky.

'Aw, shit!' Carter snarled, and thrust the Colt back into the holster. 'You ain't worth wastin' another bullet on.'

He swung away from the three dead and one injured and lashed a kick at Yancy, the toe of his boot slamming into the other boy's belly, turning him over and sprawling him out on his back.

Yancy shrieked his pain and gasped: 'Why you do that to me, Johnnie?'

'Why?' Carter strode angrily over to the side of his wagon, knocked the top off a water barrel and used a dipper to ladle out some of the contents. He took two sips and then threw the water into his face. 'I don't know why! I don't know the why of any of this! Ask Mr short-ass friggin' Steele. He acts like he knows every damn thin' about every damn thin'!'

'Only God is that smart, kid,' Steele said as he pushed two fresh bullets into the empty chambers of the Colt Hartford cylinder.

The three girls had climbed down off the Conestogas. Trudy Shelby glared hatefully at Carter and then hurried over to where Yancy was trying to sit up, groaning and clutching at his punished stomach. Veronica Carter just stood and looked helplessly around. Sara Yancy approached Steele.

'There wasn't no time to ask Him what to do!' John Carter snarled. 'Like you had no friggin' time after you got your horse shot out from under you!'

'That's right, John!' his sister agreed. 'He killed that man quicker than the blinkin' of an eye!'

'Before they surrendered!' Sara blurted, stopping four feet short of where Steele was getting painfully to his feet again. She whirled as she voiced her defence of the Virginian, so that he had just a glimpse of her face glowering with rage before she put her tension-rigid back to him. 'You shot down men who'd thrown away their guns! Two of them after they'd put their hands up!'

'I know that,' Yancy said miserably as he was helped upright by Trudy. 'When I saw 'em laying there, that's what made me sick to my stomach.'

Shelby quickly holstered his gun, almost as if he felt this would reduce his share of the blame for what had happened.

'Shit on that!' Carter snarled, brushing droplets of water and beads of sweat off his face with a shirt sleeve. 'They had guns on us first! And they fired the first friggin' shot! If we hadn't gone at them they'd likely have blasted us the same way they done to your horse, Steele!'

'Hey, that's right!' Phil Shelby said grimly. 'And it was Steele brung us right up to this place, wasn't it? Seems to me he ain't got no reason to act high and mighty with us, Johnnie!'

'You people,' the lieutenant rasped. 'You got anythin' aboard those wagons that'll ease the pain in my guts?'

'Why should we do anythin' for you, mister?' Carter demanded brutally.

'Nothin',' Sara said, looking from the wounded man to Steele and then back again. 'When we started out we just never counted on anythin' like this happenin'.'

'A smoke then?' the man asked, his dirt streaked face seeming to shrink thinner with each moment of agony he endured, the eyes appearing to sink deeper into their dark sockets. 'I could sure use a cigarette.'

'Roll him one, Johnnie!' Sara commanded.

'Like hell I will!'

'Here,' Phil Shelby offered, taking some ready rolled cigarettes from his shirt pocket and stooping down in front of the wounded man, extending them toward him.

The lieutenant took one, but the blood on his hand soaked through the paper. So Shelby put one between the parched and cracked lips, struck a match on his boot and lit the tobacco.

'Is there nothin' we can do for him, Adam?' Sara asked softly. 'He looks so awful.'

'Better than he did a while ago,' the Virginian replied.

She blinked her confusion. 'Better?'

'Without a rifle in his hands.'

CHAPTER FIVE

'I SWEAR to God, mister. I never knew Sergeant Brant had a bullet in his rifle,' the lieutenant groaned. 'He told me he'd used all his ammo the same as Brown and Winkler. And me.'

They were all sitting in the deep shade of the defile, waiting for the man with the bullet in his belly to die. Despite being sheltered from the direct glare of the sun, the area between the high rocks was still hot. Almost painfully hot. But the youngsters were able to ignore their own suffering: to put it into perspective by looking at the dying man and realising how lucky they were.

Adam Steele simply took the discomfort of the suffocating heat for granted as he chewed on jerked beef and drank three cups of coffee. The lieutenant was in no condition to eat or drink and the runaway kids felt they would all get as sick as Al Yancy had been after they had seen the dying man's agony and heard his screams as he was lifted into the shade. The Virginian had taken care of the already dead to the extent of dragging the corpses unceremoniously deep into the defile. Out of sight of where Veronica Carter lit a fire. Soon, the stench of decomposing flesh would permeate the oven-hot air, but by then the wagon train would be back on the trail.

The lieutenant spoke without being asked for an explanation, to end a silence that had lasted for perhaps fifteen minutes.

'What on?' Al Yancy asked, pale-faced and weak looking after the violent bout of nausea. 'What were you shootin' at?'

The bare chested man, who was propped up with his back against the rock face and had a blanket from the Carter wagon draped over his middle to hide the wound, nodded to Phil Shelby. The boy with the tightly curled hair and untidy moustache hurried to light a cigarette, take the remnants of the last one off the lieutenant's lower lip and place the fresh smoke in position.

All the youngsters were as anxious as this to meet the wishes of the man: their attitudes contrite, their expressions doleful. But since moving him into the defile all he ever needed was a constant supply of cigarettes. And Shelby was the lucky one. Lucky in that he had a plentiful fund of the makings and the others were patently jealous that only he was ministering to the needs of the lieutenant.

'Redskins, son. Bunch of renegade Paiutes with two bottle thirsts and one bottle heads.'

The kids began to fire questions at the fatally injured man, seizing eagerly on the fact that he apparently needed to talk and anxious to give him subjects to talk on: which just might help to take his mind off his suffering.

Steele glanced at the lieutenant and guessed that the end was near. The hollow-cheeked, sunken-eyed, dirt-ingrained, heavily stubbled face was composed. His agony had reached that point at which it was not possible for his brain to recognise anything of a greater intensity. He might have passed out then. Or, as had actually happened, detached his mind from his physical sensations—by delving deep into the back of it to consider recollections of better times. And some that in their own way were worse.

'No, we weren't out on patrol, little lady,' he said in response to a question from the full-bodied Veronica Carter. And was even able to draw back his thin lips from his yellow stained teeth to show a bitter smile. 'You people don't have anythin' to fear from the army or the law for what you did. We were on the run. Broke out of a cage wagon that was takin' us to Leavenworth to serve our sentences. That was down on the Hastings Cut-Off south of the Great Salt Lake. Figured to make for the Canadian border. Never did make it.'

He had started out speaking strongly but his voice got weaker by the moment. Or perhaps he was merely speaking softly, now unaware of his audience or choosing to ignore them. Voicing his thoughts.

'Just the clothes we had when we broke out of that cage on wheels. And Winchesters we took from those dumb guards. Two of them not fully loaded. Always either hungry or thirsty. A lot of the time both. Them Paiutes would have seen we had nothing to steal if they hadn't been drunk. But the bastards jumped us for sure. Must have been a dozen of them at the start.' He vented a short, high-pitched giggle. 'Got four of them stone dead. Three at least trailin' blood when they high-tailed it away. But used all our ammo seein' off the bastards. None left to hunt with. Had to eat berries. Except for that one time old Jed Winkler tickled some trout. Raw fish don't taste at all bad when a man's real hungry, you know.'

He was still talking to himself, staring across the glowing ashes of the fire that would probably die at about the same time as he did, through the slow rising smoke and out over the brightly sunlit Blue Mountains foothills.

'How far away did it happen?' the skinny, lanky, long-haired Trudy Shelby asked.

'What's that?' The lieutenant snapped his head from side to side, momentarily surprised and confused by the fact that seven people were hearing what he said.

'The Indians,' the spotty-faced girl augmented, and her anxiety was transmitted to the rest of the youngsters, 'How far off are they?'

'Oh, fifty miles or so,' the man replied, after a short pause for thought. 'Week ago they hit us. More or less. A man can lose track of time. Lose his sense of direction, too. And not cover too many miles in a day. When he doesn't eat the way he should.'

His cigarette had gone out and he did not ask for another.

'What were you going to serve time for, feller?' Steele said as the youngsters enjoyed the relief of knowing the remnants of the band of drunken Indians were far off.

'Thought you said it wasn't done for a man to ask other people's business out here, mister?' John Carter growled.

'Rules are for breaking, kid,' the Virginian answered. 'But before you can break them, you have to know them.'

'Does it matter, Adam?' Sara wanted to know, unable to tear her gaze away from the pathetically diminished form of a man who had obviously once been a strong, handsome army officer. 'They were hungry and sick. It seems to me that it don't matter what...'

'Raped a kid on her thirteenth birthday, little lady,' the lieutenant cut in, and grimaced as the first wave of a new sea of pain broke over him. 'Snotnose daughter of the snotnose major who commanded our post. Jesus Christ was that kid a bitch. Got everythin' she wanted from her Pa and figured everyone else oughta treat her like she was some foreign royalty or somethin'. Just because old Jed Winkler accidentally spat on her dress that time, that bitch made up a story about him. Told the major old Jed put his hands on her. Everybody at the post knew that wasn't true but the lousy sonofabitchin' major wasn't about to disbelieve his little girl. And all old Jed did was spit. Men are always spittin', ain't that so? And you don't always take much notice of where you spit at.'

'So you raped a thirteen year old girl?' Sara Yancy asked.

'Sure did. Me and old Jed and Brant and Harry Brown. Wasn't nobody on that post was goin' to stand around and watch old Jed get spread on a wagon wheel and whipped for somethin' he didn't do. So they was all lookin' the other way when we took the major and his bitch of a daughter out into the timber. And we laid more than hands on her.'

'Oh, my God!' Sara groaned.

The lieutenant was by turns grimacing in response to the searing agony in his belly and leering his enjoyment of the memories which came vividly into his mind.

'Planned on killin' the major after it was over, but them sonsofbitches that agreed to keep their backs turned on us got cold feet. Moved into the timber and stopped us doin' that. Then give evidence against us at the court martial.'

'You're friggin' savages!' Veronica Carter rasped. 'You deserve to friggin' die!'

'What the court figured, little lady,' the lieutenant hissed, and pushed both hands down under the blanket to claw at the bullet hole with its surrounding circle of black, congealed blood. 'But the major figured that would be too easy for us. Had enough pull to get the death sentence reduced to life. Life! Jesus Christ! Reduced to life! In an army prison! That is one bad joke!'

'I'm glad the others are dead and you're gonna die, mister!' Trudy Shelby flung down at him as she sprang to her feet. 'The world's gonna be a better place without you!'

'How would you know?' Steele asked, just before the lieutenant gaped his mouth wide and uttered a piercingly shrill scream that drew every pair of eyes toward him. In time to see him press his shoulders back against the rock, push his feet to the ground and arch his body. The blanket fell off him and the kids either snapped their gazes away or covered their eyes: as the man's powerful response to the abrupt onslaught of unbearable agony caused the black crusting of dried blood to burst open and a jet of bright crimson to erupt.

Then he died, the scream curtailed and his body collapsing back to the ground, chin resting on his chest and hands flopping down to either side, palms upwards.

'You should have let us kill him like the others!' Phil Shelby snarled. 'At least it was easy and quick for them.'

'No!' his sister blurted. 'He had it comin'! They should all have gone through dyin' the hard way!'

Now that he was inert and silent they could all look at him, repulsed by what they saw but able to calm their emotions. Then Sara looked up at Steele as he rose to his feet and kicked some dusty dirt on to the ashes of the fire.

'You know somethin', Adam?'

'Reckon you're going to tell me.'

'All this has left you cold, ain't it? Apart from when the shootin' was goin' on, you've been like the wooden Indian that stands outside Mr Coker's cigar store in Shelterville.'

'That's because he's what I told you he was, woman!' Carter said with a scowl. 'He's a professional killer who enjoys his work. When he ain't shootin' a gun, he's like a friggin' fish outta water.'

The boy had got to his feet and now he strode angrily around the dead fire and the dead man, heading for the wagons.

'Look out, Johnnie!' Al Yancy yelled.

But the warning came too late for Carter to evade the punch that Steele threw at him: gave him time to swing his eyes in their sockets and see the gloved fist coming toward him, but no chance to duck or pull back his head. The blow caught him on the side of the jaw and he went down like a suddenly deflated bag of air, eyes glazed and face drained of colour beneath the light tan of his skin.

The Virginian had attacked fast and without any kind of warning. Perhaps had allowed his anger to glint in his dark eyes at the moment the blow struck home. Then, as Carter started to fall, his face reverted to the impassive set which it had displayed before.

'Adam, why did you do that?' Sara asked shrilly, hurrying across to where the stunned boy was shaking his head. She dropped to her knees beside him, but he brushed away the comfort she offered with her hands. Used one of his own to explore the swelling already risen on his jaw, and glared his enmity up at Steele.

The Virginian looked around at everyone else and saw they were formed into a pack again, sharing in Carter's pain and humiliation and staring at the man responsible for it with varying degrees of the same expression worn by the boy on the ground.

'He overstepped the mark is why,' Steele replied levelly,

continuing to rake his eyes from left to right to ensure everyone knew they were all included in what he had to say. 'Just like that thirteen-year-old girl did when she accused a cavalryman of doing something he never did.'

'Adam, you can't make out...'

'Shut up and listen!' he interrupted Sara Yancy. 'And maybe learn enough to make you turn tail and head for home.'

Phil Shelby was in process of lighting one of the cigarettes he had saved by the lieutenant dying. 'One of the reasons we left there was to get away from friggin' lectures by people figured they knew what was best for us, mister!' he growled.

Steele remained calm at this interruption and shook his head. 'Not a lecture, kid. A piece of advice. About people who wear guns for a better reason than it makes them feel older.'

'You're as old as the friggin' hills anyway!' John Carter taunted, and sounded and looked childishly young.

'Shut up!' Sara snapped at him.

'Guns are for killing,' the Virginian continued as if the exchange had not taken place. But suddenly found himself feeling as elderly as Carter had said. 'It's the reason they were invented. For killing living things to eat first off, I guess. But it didn't take long for people to find out they killed other people just as well as animals. Now the reason I hit Carter was to keep myself from blowing his head off.' He raised the Colt Hartford from down at his side to cant it to his shoulder. 'And I would have enjoyed doing that. Because he's been riling me an awful lot since I tied myself in with you kids. Same as I enjoyed killing Brant because he tried to kill me. Wasn't any money involved. Wouldn't have earned a cent by putting Carter down in a way he'd never have gotten up again.'

Sara got to her feet and nodded her head in a gesture of understanding. But there was confusion in her big green eyes. 'All right, Adam. I guess we all get your message on that. But why should you not being a professional gunman make us want to go home?'

He pursed his lips and sighed. 'I'm not through yet.'

'I'm sorry.'

'Told you at the start you'd all have cause to be that. But now I'm not so sure you'll have the time. Could be your folks will be the sorry ones, when they come to look at whatever place you're buried in.'

'Shit on that!' Shelby rasped. 'We took care of three of them friggin' rapists while you was still crawlin' around in the dust after your horse got shot from under you! We can take care of ourselves. Right Johnnie?'

'Hear the man out, Phil,' Carter said evenly.

Steele nodded his acknowledgement of the invitation to finish. 'You hear what he called those four fellers?'

'But they admitted it, mister,' Al Yancy said, a little exasperated. 'Leastways, the lieutenant did. And there was no point in him lying.'

'Right, kid. No point in him lying about the false charge laid by the major's daughter, either. Or about her being a snotnose bitch toward all the men serving on that post . . .'

'But, Adam!' Sara cried, shocked again. 'You can't condone four men's assault on a helpless little girl! And they made her father watch them do it, for God's sake!'

'I can't condone it or condemn it, miss,' he replied and this time she gave no indication of disappointment that he had not used her given name. 'Because I don't know the facts that led up to them doing it. And until you learn not to make up your minds before you know all you're ever going to have a chance to know, then the world outside Shelterville is no place for you kids.'

He swung around and went out of the defile and over to the dead gelding. A swarm of flies lifted angrily off the wound in the horse's chest as he squatted down to unfasten the saddle cinch. Then he hauled the saddle and bedroll out from under the carcase, took of the bridle and reins and carried all this over to the black stallion of Eric Shelby.

While he was engaged in this chore of switching his gear from the dead horse to the living one, he could hear the youngsters talking together in the shaded defile. Mostly their voices reached his ears as a low keyed mumbling sound. But occasionally anger caused somebody to shout.

He had been sitting astride the new horse for about five minutes, gazing out over the sun bright landscape from under the brim of his hat, when the group emerged and advanced upon him like a delegation seeking peace. All of them showed expressions which were a strange mixture of reluctance and determination—blended with some deep-seated anxiety.

'Adam,' Sara Yancy said, despite the fact that he was looking directly at her, fully expecting that she would again be their spokeswoman. 'We're much obliged to you and we'll keep in mind what you told us.'

'Fine.'

'But we're not goin' back. We're gonna make lives for ourselves outside of Shelterville. And we reckon we can do that. I guess if we ever thought about it, we knew from the start it wasn't gonna be easy. But we think we can learn how to do it.' She tried a wan smile, discovered the expression felt good on her face and broadened it into a grin. 'And it can't all be as bad as this, can it?'

He smiled, but less brightly. A little ruefully, even, as he swept his gaze over the bunch of kids and realised he had been too hard on them. Recalling again that he had been young and inexperienced once: had led a spoiled and privileged life before being thrust, green and naive, into what seemed like another world.

'I always say you have to take the rough with the smooth, Sara. And it's the rough parts that make you appreciate the smooth.'

'So you'll stay with us? If we accept folks for what they are and don't do anythin' before we check with you.'

'Why not? I'm looking for the same thing you people are.

No reason to expect I'm more likely to find it in any other direction than the one we're heading in.'

'What about the dead, Mr Steele?' Al Yancy asked, his spectacles rising and falling over the bridge of his nose.

'What about them, son?'

'Didn't we oughta bury them? Like we did Phil and Trudy's Pa?'

'Depends how bad you feel about killing them.'

'You're not gonna plant the one you blasted?' Phil Shelby wanted to know.

Steele briefly tipped back his head to squint up into the dazzlingly blue sky, against which a half dozen buzzards were lazily circling. 'Nature always takes care of its own, if we allow it.'

Some of the youngsters shuddered, obviously at a vivid mental image of the big birds swooping down to tear at the flesh of the dead soldiers.

'I say we allow it,' John Carter muttered as he absently ran his fingertips over the now blackened swelling on the side of his jaw. Then he grinned at the Virginian. 'Shows I've learned a lesson, Mr Steele, don't it? I may not like what them creatures have in mind to do, but it needs doin'.'

'Well, I think it's horrible!' his sister countered.

'So don't think about it, Ron,' Sara said wearily. 'We all agreed to do what Adam tells us. And it looks like he's ready to leave right now?'

'We all are,' Carter announced, took hold of Sara's upper arm and steered her toward the lead wagon.

Yancy escorted the Shelby girl in the direction of his Conestoga which was last in line and Shelby headed for the centre wagon. This left the short, full-bodied, round-faced Veronica Carter standing alone in front of the mounted Steele. For a few moments, she continued to express her distaste for leaving the corpses to be scavenged by the buzzards. Then she realised she was standing in isolation and showed the

Virginian a brittle smile before running to catch up with her beau.

'They're God's creatures just like us, ain't they?' she called back over her shoulder.

'All set, Mr Steele!' Carter yelled after he had looked along the side of the wagon to check that everyone was aboard the other two Conestogas.

The Virginian heeled his horse forward and heard the wagons creak and clatter into movement behind him.

'Eat well, you ugly black bastards!' Carter called as the buzzards began to spiral downwards.

Steele raised some saliva into his mouth and made to spit. But glanced to his left and saw Sara Yancy on the periphery of his vision, gazing sorrowfully at him. He swallowed and growled to himself: 'Stick close to us and you'll eat regular.'

CHAPTER SIX

Trouble stayed away from the lumbering wagons and the lone horseback rider for several days as they continued to push south east at an unhurried pace over the rugged terrain of the Continental Divide. They travelled through the dusty heat of long days and slept close to a roaring fire through each short, chillingly cold night. Sometimes a wind would curl in over the northern ridges, hurling stinging dust into their faces during the day or causing them to curl up tight beneath their blankets at nights.

Nobody complained about anything and everyone did his or her chores willingly. The boys did not use obscenities so much and the girls ceased to blaspheme. Steele became an integral member of the group instead of the suffered outsider he had once been: by responding to their initially tentative efforts to emulate Sara's easy-going friendliness toward him. He and the girl continued to call each other by their given names. The others referred to him as 'sir' or 'Mr Steele'. He called them 'son' or 'miss'.

Thus did a genuine respect for each other develop between the man and the youngsters and a set of rules and code of behaviour become established without any need for discussion. The Virginian was in his element and the youngsters realised this and showed their trust in him by following his example or asking his advice.

At first he found this disconcerting and not just because it was a complete turn about from the situation which had once existed. Primarily he was troubled by his own change of attitude rather than theirs. For it stressed his age in comparison with the youth of the group, and made him feel like a lecher whenever he looked at Sara Yancy. It also increased his awareness that, apart from this age difference between the girl and himself, she was promised to John Carter: a boy who was now probably more amicably disposed toward Steele than everyone with the exception of Sara.

But gradually, as the days and nights passed, he came to terms with his feelings. By simply ignoring them. Something he had done countless times before. Not always with such ease as on this occasion when the subject of his wanting understood his problem and helped him to handle it. By going out of her way to stay out of his way: and by emphasising her attachment to Carter — holding his hand while they rode the Conestoga, serving him first at the mealtimes when she did the cooking and placing her bedroll close to his at night camps.

Nobody could fail to notice such actions nor to hear the terms of endearment which Sara used with increasing frequency. And a lot of good humoured ribbing went on which Carter and Sara accepted in the spirit it was given.

Nobody saw the looks which were exchanged — maybe as much as twice a day or only every other day — between Adam Steele and the girl. The secret looks that each spoke a thousand words and gave the lie to the relationship between Sara and Carter. Looks which acknowledged acceptance of a situation that should not have been but which had to be — neither the man nor the girl knowing quite why.

It was at the dawning of a new day which seemed set to be as hot and dusty as the many gone before when a sound roused Steele from the shallow level of sleep that allowed him to rest and renew his energy and yet left part of his mind alert, on guard to warn him of the first indication of potential danger.

He snapped open his eyes and looked at the sky which was just beginning to change from star sprinkled black to featureless grey. For long moments his ears picked up only the familiar gurgling sounds of the Snake River which ran shallow and narrow beyond where the three wagons were parked. Then he heard the sleep noises of the six youngsters who had all now taken to placing their bedrolls in pairs like Sara and John Carter.

He raised his head and then his back up off the blanket on the ground.

The camp was on the north bank of the Snake, in the lee of a brush covered rise which had offered some protection from the cold breeze that was blowing when he called a halt to the trek last night. There was no wind this morning, and out beyond the broad river bed with the tiny stream trickling down its centre, he could see nothing that moved. Just an empty wilderness of rolling hill country that revealed not a single sign that man had ever set foot on it. Grassy rises with here and there areas of exposed rock where many winds, far more powerful than that of the previous night, had eroded the life giving soil. Featured with clumps of brush and stands of stunted trees, all of them bent toward the south as further testament of the strength and invariable direction of the winds.

Steele rose to his feet, gripping the Colt Hartford in both gloved hands and allowing the blankets to drop around his ankles. He raked his wary eyes to the north and south, able to see the day become lighter by the moment in advance of the sun's leading arc.

'It's almost frighteningly beautiful, ain't it, Adam?' Sara said.

She was right. The stillness and emptiness of the vast landscape to the south, east and west was awesome. Perhaps because in the crystal clarity of the air in these dawning moments it was as if it were possible to see to the very end of the earth: and if a man — or a woman — were able to discount the presence of those who unwittingly shared the vastness and the serenity, they could imagine themselves totally alone and in command of everything spread before them. And it was all too much for the human mind to comprehend.

Steele looked back at her as she murmured the comment, and saw her taking pains not to make any sounds which might disturb the others as she eased up from her bedroll and started around the ashes of the fire to approach him. She was displaying that special brand of sleep dishevelled beauty he had seen on other mornings. But this morning it was a little frightening, too. For the Shelby and Carter brothers and sisters and her own brother were soundly asleep. Which meant that she and the Virginian were to all intents and purposes alone with each other for the first time since he rode out of the pine trees. With no need to exchange secret glances. And the way she looked at him made it patently clear that she welcomed the situation.

'You could be right to be afraid of it, Sara,' he replied, snatching his gaze away from her face to rake it once more over the seemingly limitless expanse of rolling hills.

'Why?' She gasped the word and caught hold of his forearm, her fingers digging into his flesh beneath the shirt sleeve.

He felt a stab of sexual pleasure at her touch and snatched a sidelong glance at her profile. Then tightened his mouthline and called himself a fool. The girl looked genuinely afraid as she peered out over the hills beyond the wagons, the hobbled horses and the trickling stream. There was no hint in her attitude to suggest that she was making a pretence — faking an emotion to give her an excuse to get this close to him.

'Thought I heard something out there.'

'Somethin'?'

'Can't say what. A sound that woke me up.'

He felt even more of a fool. A very old fool. Like he was the one who was pretending: lying to this young girl so that she would do precisely what she was doing. It was crazy. He had never had any intention of causing such a situation to develop when he responded instinctively to the sound that had not been repeated. So why the hell should he feel so guilty?

'Adam.'

He turned his head, then felt the cool fingers of her free

hand on his cheek, his ear and the nape of his neck. As she pulled his face down on to hers. Their lips met and his guilt expanded as he experienced the pressure of one of her breasts against his upper arm.

They were standing awkwardly, he sideways-on to her with only his head turned toward her. She holding his arm and neck. He gripping the rifle across his belly. He wanted desperately to release the Colt Hartford, take her in his arms and hold her so that the entire length of her body was pressed to his. There were a thousand reasons why he should not and only one why he should. And out of the turmoil in his mind he plucked that one reason for positive action and got as far as starting to loosen his grip on the rifle.

Then the man roared: 'You filthy little harlot!'

A horse snorted as Sara let go with both hands and sprang backwards, a cry of fear venting from her lips as an expression of horror took command of her lovely face.

Steele suddenly realised it was such an equine sound which had roused him from sleep. But it had come from a greater distance. Which he could understand. But from a different direction, he was certain. And this was disturbing.

'My father,' Sara hissed. 'Shit, what a friggin' lousy time for that sonofabitch to show up!'

The Virginian had part of a second in which to be shocked by the girl's language, then devoted all his attention to the two men who were advancing down the slope above where the other youngsters were coming awake, disturbed by the enraged words of one of the newcomers.

Both men were in their late fifties or early sixties. Tall men with broad shoulders and thick waists. Warmly dressed for night riding. Travel stained. Sitting astride fine looking stallions which had been ridden long and hard.

'It ain't what you're thinkin', Pa!' Sara shouted, sidling away from Steele as the two riders neared the foot of the slope. And her brother and friends got up from their bedrolls, eyeing the newcomers anxiously and then looking suspiciously at the Virginian and the girl.

'What you doin' here, Dad?' Veronica Carter asked.

'Don't ask damn fool questions, girl!' the silver-haired, narrow-eyed, short-necked Douglas Carter snarled as he reined in his horse and dismounted slowly and carefully, grimacing from the pains of aching muscles.

'We've come to take you crazy kids back home where you belong, that's what!' Yancy snarled, glaring at his son, the Shelby and Carter youngsters and finally at Sara. 'Just hope we ain't caught up with you too late.'

He had even more trouble than Carter in getting down off his horse because he had a stiff right leg that would bend hardly at all. When he finally made it to the ground he kneaded the fleshy thigh of that leg with both hands.

'Too late?' Veronica Carter asked, frowning her lack of understanding.

'Look at yourself, girl!' her father growled, his dark eyes glaring his anger. 'Dressed in a man's clothes but lookin' in no way like any man ever did! Sara the same! And Gertrude Shelby! Travellin' with young fellers. Sleepin' nights with . . .'

'We seen with our own eyes what my brazen slut of a daughter was gettin' up to!' Yancy cut in. 'Indulgin' in the sins of the flesh with that evil-intentioned molester! Why, if I was just five years younger I'd take off my coat and beat the hide off him!'

The Virginian had seen that the elderly newcomers posed no threat: unless Yancy's blustering words spurred John Carter into attempting to carry out what the old man had admitted he was past doing. But although the Carter boy was tense and sullen, he seemed to be more concerned with the arrival of his father and Yancy than with what had been happening between his girl and Steele.

So the Virginian turned his back on the camp to again concentrate his entire attention on the land spread to the east, south and west. Behind him the youngsters were yelling at the elderly men and Yancy and Doug Carter were snarling back at them. Anger was high and rising higher, but not a single obscenity or blasphemy was used.

Steele moved away from the area of noise and movement — as Sara lit a fresh fire on the ashes of the old and set a coffee pot to boil — and climbed up on to one of the Conestoga tail-gates. The additional height allowed him to see a little further out over the wilderness and a little deeper into the hollows between the hills on the other side of the river. Then the sun showed the curve of its leading arc above the eastern horizon and the shaft of its light served to emphasise the emptiness and stillness of the landscape over which Steele raked his eyes.

Yet he was certain a horse had snorted out there somewhere. Five, maybe ten minutes ago. That was the sound which had woken him up. Not made by the horse of Carter or Yancy because the two men had ridden into camp from the north. Nor by one of the horses hobbled beyond the line of parked wagons. They were too close.

No, this horse had been out there. A long way out, maybe, the sound it made carried a great distance through the still and otherwise silent air of the dawn.

A wild horse? An animal lost and wandering, abandoned by its owner or vice versa? Unlikely. For there had been just the single sound of the snort, then the animal had been silent. Probably silenced — by a rider.

Steele jumped down from the rear of the wagon and moved up the slope, electing to go around the camp rather than through it: not wanting to stir up another shouting match now that everyone had calmed — were sitting and squatting close to the fire, talking quietly and for the most part one at a time while they waited for the coffee pot to steam.

'Is somethin' wrong, Adam?' Sara called to him. 'Surely it was Pa and Mr Yancy you heard?'

She spoke for the sake of saying something to someone she

could rely on to listen and respond. For although she was in the thick of the group by the fire, she seemed somehow detached. Her misbehaviour had been dealt with and she was apparently being left to stew in her own juice while the men spoke sternly to the rest of the youngsters: who listened as if they were already halfway convinced that they were hearing sense.

'Out here nothing is ever really sure,' he replied.

'Pay attention, girl!' her father snapped, cutting across something Doug Carter was saying. 'And speak when you're spoke to! Not at all to that . . .' He searched his mind for an expletive to describe his opinion of the Virginian and one that his religious beliefs would allow him to use. But if he thought of such a word, it was the utter coldness in Steele's eyes when the two men briefly locked gazes that caused Carter to finish: '. . . man!'

Then Steele started up the rise in back of the river bank, ignoring the group by the fire and shooting constant glances back across his shoulder as he gained more and more height. Not until he was at the crest of the low hill did he look directly down toward the foot of the slope, sensing worried eyes watching him. Two pairs. The green ones of Sara Yancy. And the much older, much wiser blue ones of Doug Carter. This while Yancy senior was talking fast and on a rising note to the other youngsters — slapping a thigh and occasionally punching one fisted hand into the palm of the other to stress the points he was making.

'Steele, what's wrong?' the elder Carter yelled.

A fusilade of rifle shots filled the sudden silence which his shouted words had brought to the river bank. And John Carter's head seemed to explode, as if his brain had suddenly become black powder and a match had been struck too close to his ear. But it was not flames and smoke which leapt away from the boy's head as he powered up into a half crouch, spun around and then pitched into the fire. Instead, gouts of blood, chunks of flesh and fragments of bone. Displaced and sent flying through the now noise-filled, warming early morning air by at least four bullets which tunnelled into his face and burst free at the back of his head.

The Virginian looked away from the chaos which the gunfire had created in the camp and saw the men responsible for it. Eight of them. Indians. The right number to be the survivors of the band of Paiutes which had attacked the four hapless escaped army prisoners. Sitting astride ponies which they heeled viciously into a flat out gallop now that the initial volley of rifle shots had been fired. Up to the crest of the rise just across the river and down the slope to the bank. Firing wildly as they came. Their mouths pulled wide to vent high pitched whoops of excitement. Ponies snorting, unshod hooves thundering on the grass of the slope and bank, then the dried mud of the broad river bed before stream water was sprayed shoulder high around the attacking braves.

John Carter had been unlucky. It was perhaps a million-to-one chance that so many bullets fired over such a range in the first burst of rifle fire had found the single target of his head. While the other flying lead fell short, went high or angled to left and right: leaving the rest of the people at the fire unscathed and able to scurry for cover.

Steele wasted no time on watching the actions which accompanied the screams and shouts which rose up from the camp site. Instead, hurled himself to the ground and drew a bead on the line of attacking Indians. Naked to the waist braves with buckskin leggings and moccasins. Not wearing warpaint, but with their faces and bodies streaked by dirt which had been spread into strange patterns by old sweat.

He waited until they hit the water, aware of the danger that one of the wildly fired shots from the Paiutes' repeaters might cause John Carter's misfortune to reach out and brush him. But also conscious of the advantage which lay with the Indians. Eight battle hardened warriors, each of them armed with a repeater rifle. Who had surprised and caused panic among a group of whites. Killed one of them to even up the number, but the numbers were not important. A bunch of kids with three Navy Colts between them. A couple of ageing men who had ridden into camp with single shot Sharps in their rifle boots. And one man with a five shot Colt Hartford he could fire faster than most men could trigger bullets from a Winchester.

So the Virginian could be sure only of himself and his own abilities and he waited patiently, to pick his target and be sure of hitting it. Then he squeezed the trigger. And heard the report of his rifle matched by the deeper sounding cracks of two others. Saw three Paiute braves fling their arms high to the sides and flip backwards over the rumps of their galloping ponies.

As the trio of Indians with blood on their filthy chests crashed into the stream, Steele thumbed back the hammer of the Colt Hartford and sent a second shot cracking down toward the depleted line of attackers. And grunted his satisfaction as the man he aimed at was unseated from the bare back of his pony and toppled off to the side, blood spouting from a hole in his side and then erupting a few moments later from his mouth.

The four survivors were in cover by then, having crossed the open river bed and steered their mounts into a tight turn: headed for the line of three parked wagons and leapt to the ground.

Steele spared another glance for the scene directly at the foot of the slope. The Paiutes had got lucky with some of their wild shots. Which was bad luck for the mounts of the elder Yancy and Carter. And three of the horses from the wagon teams.

The dead and wounded animals were sprawled out on their sides, totally inert or struggling frantically to rise.

Carter and Yancy, their Sharps rifles reloaded, were making

use of the cover provided by their dead horses: stretched out prone and raking the rifle barrels from side to side in search of a target.

On the other side of the fire the youngsters had closed up into a group near to where the corpse of John Carter lay, having been hauled out of the flames. The three girls were flat to the ground, face down and hands clawed, like they were trying to drag themselves into and through the soil on which the grass grew. While Phil Shelby and Al Yancy invited death to claim them. They were down on their knees, but with thighs and backbones ramrod straight as they swung to left and right, both arms thrust out in front of them, hands wrapped around the butts of their revolvers. From above and behind them, the Virginian was unable to see the faces of the two boys. But he could hear their shrill voices between the reports of the revolvers and the louder cracks of rifle fire.

'You killed Johnnie, you friggin' bastard redskins!'

'Oh, my God, what a friggin, stinkin' mess!'

'Frig it, frig it, frig it!'

'You bastards, you bastards, you bastards!'

Sobs punctuated the enraged shrieks. The boys' heads shook from side to side faster than they swung their guns. So that the bullets were unaimed — thudding into the timber of the wagon sides or cracking out over the river bed to tunnel harmlessly into the far bank.

His own lips pursed to form the shape of an obscenity he did not voice, Adam Steele wrenched his gaze away from where the youngsters mindlessly courted death with no reason other than hysteria for what they were doing. And forced himself not to look again at where the trio of girls lay. For they were sprawled in attitudes which could be caused by terror or death. And he was not yet ready to find out which it was in the case of Sara Yancy. Because he did not trust himself to react any differently to the two revenge crazy boys if it should be that the girl was dead.

Two of the Paiute braves were in the lead wagon. The two other were crouched by the rear wheel of the centre Conestoga. Steele could not see them but he had seen the direction the Indians took when they leapt from their slowing ponies and now puffs of muzzle smoke revealed their positions. The bullets that crashed out from the Winchesters and cracked through the drifting smoke of previous gunfire were either totally wild or triggered with only token attempts at drawing a bead on targets. For, despite the stupidity of the two boys who raked their revolvers back and forth and fired them in the heat of rage, the bullets that were exploded from the chambers of the Colts served to force the braves to keep their heads down.

Which allowed Doug Carter to power to his feet and sprint for the fire.

A Paiute at the side of the centre wagon tried to draw a bead on the running man and Yancy squeezed off a shot from his Sharps. The Indian was hit in the shoulder by the heavy calibre bullet and the impact sent him sprawling backward across the grassy bank of the Snake. Which brought him into the range of vision of the Virginian. The Colt Hartford kicked its recoil against Steele's armpit and the brave, who had started to sit up, was flung back full length to the ground, blood gushing from his throat and the nape of his neck.

Yancy looked up the hill at Steele and gave a nod of approval. He had already discarded his own rifle and snatched up Carter's identical model.

'Shit, it's empty!' the man's bespectacled son roared.

'Well, friggin' re-load, you crazy sonofabitch!' Phil Shelby snarled.

His gun rattling empty had served to jerk the taller, thicker set boy out of rage which had gripped him since John Carter was killed. And now he went full length to the ground and rolled on to his side to offer less of a target to the Paiute Indians as he fumbled fresh bullets out of his gun belt. But with rage gone, fear took its place: filling his mind as full as the former emotion and acting to block it just as effectively to rational thought. Or at least to more than one such thought at a time. Thus, as he yelled the instruction to his friend, he discovered he was trying to push unfired rounds into the chambers of his own revolver before he had extracted the expended shell cases.

'Frig it!' he screamed, then: 'Oh Jesus!' as he looked up and saw Al Yancy corkscrewing to the ground, with blood torrenting from a wound in the side of his head.

'Cover me!' Doug Carter bellowed. 'Somebody please!'

Al Yancy and Phil Shelby were not able to comply, one of them hit and the other horrified into stillness by the amount of blood pouring from his friend's head. Both with empty guns, anyway. The wounded boy's father was also helpless, having fired the single shot Sharps at the brave who exploded the damaging bullet into the head of his son. The brave now lay sprawled on his back beside the other one close to the rear wheel of the centre wagon.

Which left the two renegades who had made it into the cover of the front Conestoga. Either or both of them might even now be aiming their Winchesters out through the holes in the canvas top toward the elderly, silver-haired man racing down the gentle slope of the river bank. Whirling a blazing log around his head.

The Virginian had only three bullets left in the cylinder of the Colt Hartford. And the whole side of a big Conestoga wagon to aim at.

He powered up from where he had been sprawled in the prone position and squeezed off the first of the three bullets before he was fully erect. His glove thumb pulled back the hammer and the next shot cracked from the muzzle, leaving the gun at precisely the same moment the flaming length of timber was released by Carter.

The elderly man pitched to the ground and rolled. Steele was unable to see whether it was a defensive action or if he had been hit. Certainly, tell-tale puffs of smoke showed that both braves were still alive and firing their repeaters.

He swung the Colt Hartford a fraction to the right and expended its final bullet: curled back his lips to show his teeth in a brutal grin when he heard a cry of pain from under the wagon covering. Just before the well aimed length of wood spun in through the forward opening above the driving seat. To cause the last surviving brave to shriek in terror and take a running leap from the rear end. He hit the ground sure footed and took a few long loping strides before he came to a halt. He was on the camp side of the line of wagons, more than forty feet from where the nearest rope-bridled pony was standing, nostrils flared to sniff suspiciously at the abruptly stronger scent of smoke in the morning air. As the flaming log shared its fire with the haybales aboard the wagon and the tinder dry feed caught alight with a roar.

The pony bolted. So did the other Indian mounts which had halted nearby after their riders leapt to the ground. Steele's stallion and the surviving team horses snorted their terror and struggled fantically to shed their hobbles as the smoke of raging flames billowed across the camp, black and thick, to capture and claim as a part of itself the grey, thinner, more acrid smelling vapour of exploded bullet charges.

The brave looked around himself in abject terror: certain there was no escape and equally certain he was only a split second away from death. But then he swept his dark eyes over the same scene a second time. And laughed. An ugly, insane sound to all those who heard and saw the filthy dirty, near naked Paiute brave control his fear and start to enjoy the experience of triumph.

For the Indian had seen the man standing on the crest of the hill. The one sprawled on the ground. Another crouched behind a dead horse. Two others — younger than the rest — as exposed as the white eyes who had thrown the blazing log. One man without a weapon in his hand. The rest armed, but with empty rifles and revolvers they were hurrying to reload. With just a single bullet which would be enough, fired by an expert, to bring the battle to an end.

The Paiute raised the stock of the Winchester to his shoulder and angled the barrel up the hill toward the white eyes whose gloved hands were working the smoothest and fastest to eject a fired bullet case and insert a new round. It was the longest and most difficult shot for the brave to make, but it was as if he instinctively sensed that unless he killed this man first, his cause was bound to be lost.

And perhaps he would have blasted a fatal bullet into some vital organ of the dudishly attired Virginian before Steele had time to thumb back the hammer after shoving a single live round into a chamber of the Colt Hartford's cylinder. Had not the brave himself been cut down by a hail of bullets from a fanned gun in the hands of one of the white eyes he had not taken into account.

It was John Carter's gun which did the damage, having been dragged out of the dead boy's holster by Sara Yancy as she struggled to her feet. And she fired it in the way she had seen Carter and the other boys using their Colts back at the defile, holding it close to her hip with one hand and panning the hammer with heel of the other.

Nobody ever bothered to count how many of the six bullets from the revolver tore into the flesh of the Paiute brave. Enough anyway to send him staggering backwards into the cloud of thick black smoke that was shrouding the burning wagon. Perhaps enough in the right areas to mean that he was on the brink of dying when he emerged from the choking smoke, staring down in anger and shock at his hands, which no longer gripped the Winchester.

Then the Colt Hartford aimed by Adam Steele and the Sharps in the hands of Yancy exploded shots down the hill and across the slope. There was already blood on the brave's belly, staining the leggings enclosing one of his thighs and spilling out of his mouth to run down his jaw. But these flows were as from minor scratches compared with the great torrent of bright crimson which gushed from his chest, left of centre, as both rifle bullets tore into the Paiute's heart.

This time the impact of the shots pushed him into the billowing smoke rather than causing him to stagger. And he did not re-emerge.

'Man, did we stop him the best way there is to stop a hostile Injun, mister!' the grinning father of the Yancy youngsters yelled, rising from behind the dead horse and peering up at the Virginian.

'Yeah, feller,' Steele muttered, not loud enough for anyone else to hear. 'I reckon we just about took the heart right out of him.'

CHAPTER SEVEN

'JONAS!' Doug Carter shouted. 'Remember not the old days! We're different kinds of people now!'

The Yancy father looked suitably chastened as he turned away from the rising form of Carter. Then he saw the blood which covered one side of his son's head and he groaned his concern and threw down the Sharps to go over to the boy. But Trudy Shelby reached him first, to kneel down and press the bloodied face to her flat chest. She wailed her grief and shook her head frantically in face of the father's pleas to take a look at the boy.

Phil Shelby and Veronica Carter clasped hands and switched their horror-filled eyes between Doug Carter and Sara as the father and intended bride-to-be of John approached the virtually headless, fire scorched corpse of the boy.

The Virginian reached the foot of the hill with a fully loaded rifle and ignored the people from Shelterville in the same manner that they paid no attention to him. Until he had disappeared through the drifting smoke from the burning wagon: and beyond this fired three closely-spaced shots. That silenced the agonised sounds of a trio of wounded team horses: and triggered an hysterical outburst from the Carter girl.

'There's more of them! They're comin' to get us! To make us pay for what we done to their . . .'

A hand cracked across a cheek and as Steele came out of the smoke he saw it was Doug Carter who had slapped the panic out of his daughter: was now pointing the hand across the camp site.

'Just him takin' care of the sufferin' animals, girl!' he explained and there was a brief glimpse of previously well concealed compassion and gentleness in the way he spoke to and looked at his daughter.

'Let me take a look, girl!' Jonas Yancy snarled, his tone and expression warning of a bad spate of anger he was having trouble keeping under control. 'He's breathin' strong. Could be we can help him!'

'Go to friggin' hell!' the Shelby girl flung back, then vented a shrill wail and pressed the blood run face of Al Yancy even harder to her almost non-existent bosom when the boy made a small whimpering sound.

'If your father could hear you use that kinda language . . .'

'Damnit, Trudy!' Al Yancy complained with clear-voiced, mild anger — causing his father to halt in mid-flow — 'You'll break my glasses you ain't careful!'

The death of John Carter was somehow made easier to bear by the fact that Al Yancy was merely slightly wounded: the bullet having stunned him and erupted a great deal of blood, from a long but not very deep wound across his left temple.

The boy's recovery from apparent certain death was the first good thing to have happened on this as yet hardly started day and it was seized upon by all except one survivor of the battle with over-enthusiastic eagerness. They all wanted to help, to do everything at once: to clean away the blood, bathe the wound and dress it. The youngsters and the elderly men were able — for those first few moments of euphoria — to put from their minds the inescapable fact that one of their number would not get up and walk away from where he fell.

Steele took no part in the activity at the fireside as the protesting Al Yancy was made comfortable and it was at length decided that Trudy could attend to the injury unaided. By which time Veronica was weeping and being comforted by Phil Shelby, Sara was busying herself with making fresh coffee and Doug Carter and Jonas Yancy had taken the first step toward dealing with the body of John. They had each brought a blanket from the untidy bedrolls and draped them over the corpse.

'I'm sorry, Doug,' Yancy growled when this was done. 'You think we oughta try puttin' out the fire?'

'She's passed savin', Jonas. Sorry for John gettin' killed is all?'

'You know I don't mean that, Doug. For actin' a while back like it was a lot of years ago. And the wagons was rollin' west instead of east like now.'

'You mean that neither of you fellers is sorry the kid's dead?' Steele asked and the two men swung toward him with surprise — had obviously forgotten about him since Al Yancy had growled his intention to go on living. Which was at about the same time that the Virginian returned through the drifting smoke to where the surviving horses were hobbled among the carcases of the dead animals. Now he showed himself again. leading the black stallion by the bridle.

'He'll be missed,' the dead boy's father replied grimly. 'But not mourned. He's gone to a place far better than this one. That is what we must hope, anyway. Provided he has committed no other evils since leavin' our town, sir.'

'Even if he did, Douglas, his youth will surely be seen by God as grounds for forgiveness,' Yancy consoled.

'Sure thing, Jonas.' Carter looked from Steele to Yancy and then raked his grim-eyed gaze over the faces of the five youngsters. 'But although the Good Lord is bountiful in his loving mercy, there is a limit to his patience. Recall you children what the Reverend Turner preached of the dangers that would befall you if we went away from our town before you were of age.'

'Please, Pa, not now,' Veronica Carter complained. 'Let's get away from this place and somewhere we can bury Johnnie.'

'Yes, sir, Mr Carter, I think that is what we oughta do,' Phil Shelby agreed.

'Adam!' Sara called, when she looked up from filling a half dozen coffee cups and saw the Virginian had led the stallion across the camp and was cinching his saddle to the animal's back. 'You're not leavin'?'

'Reckon I am,' he replied evenly to her anxiously voiced query. 'You kids have got your folks with you now and family differences are none of my concern.'

'But they'll be goin' back to Shelterville, Adam!' the green eyed, short haired blonde countered quickly. 'We won't be goin' with them so we'll still need you!'

'Now listen here, girl!' her father snarled.

'No, you listen, Pa!' the girl retorted, whirling to face him and meeting his glare of anger with an expression that startled the man by its intensity. 'Me and Johnnie and Ron and Trudy and Al and Phil escaped from all that kinda crap Mr Carter was just spoutin' and the Reverend Turner was always preachin'! We said frig to all the hangin' around like angels with wings waitin' for God to spread the welcome mat out for us in heaven! And now we took the plunge and got away from that kinda life that ain't no life at all, we sure as friggin' hell ain't gonna turn around and go . . .'

'Hold your filthy, foul-mouthed tongue!' Jonas Yancy roared and lunged toward his daughter: bringing up his arm with the fist clenched.

Steele halted in the act of swinging up astride the saddle after lashing his gear into place. His rifle was firmly in the boot and he was wrongly placed to draw it in time. And the range was too long for the knife, which he could have jerked from the sheath inside the split in his pants leg, but could not be sure of sending accurately into the moving target of the man's descending arm. And it would need the searing pain of a bullet or a blade tearing into the flesh to halt Jonas Yancy's act of violence. Certainly mere words would never penetrate the fathomless depths of the rage which gripped him.

Others tried.

'You'll kill her, man!' From Douglas Carter.

'No, Pa!' Al Yancy shrieked, knocking aside Trudy's arm

as she continued to bathe the bloody furrow the bullet had ploughed across the side of his head.

'Mr Yancy!' Phil Shelby roared.

Veronica Carter screamed, looking more terrified of the man's rage than she had been of the murderous Paiutes.

Steele turned his back on the scene and closed his ears to the sounds: pleased with his own self control that allowed him to remain apart from the family trouble, just as he had said he intended to. Then, as he pushed his feet into the stirrups, took the reins in both gloved hands and turned his head to look again across the camp, he had to use every last ounce of his self-discipline to keep from using the rifle or knife. Not just to injure Jonas Yancy. But to kill him.

The man's clenched fist blow had struck his daughter on the point of the jaw, with a force that had lifted her feet clear of the ground and sent her bodily backwards through thin air. To a point more than a yard away from where she had been standing, there to collapse into an untidy heap of curled body and tangled arms and legs. Breathing raggedly and with a wet sound, as if there was blood in her throat.

'You dang fool, Jonas!' Doug Carter barked. 'You gotta have broke her jaw at least!'

Yancy seemed suddenly to shrink in size as his shoulders sagged and he began to pant for breath—the shock of the realisation of what he had done serving to exhaust him as surely as if he had just undergone some tremendous physical strain.

Carter and the Shelby brother and sister, Veronica and his bloody-faced son stared at Jonas Yancy with such intensity that the guilty man felt bound to look at each in turn, his own features expressing a greater degree of anguish with each part of a second that elapsed.

'Leave her!' Steele snarled, jerking on the reins to wheel the stallion and thudding in his heels to lunge the horse across the camp: then bringing him to a snorting halt between the unconscious girl and the group of frightened people who had complied with the Virginian's command.

'Mister, you said family affairs weren't your concern,' the silver-haired Doug Carter said huskily. 'Now I ain't denyin' that what Jonas done to his girl was wrong, but I figure he's learned his lesson. Like all these children have learned theirs too, I guess?'

He looked to his left and right, seeking words or gestures of agreement. None of the youngsters said or did anything and he chose to accept this lack of response as tacit approval.

'My boy dead and only good fortune the rest didn't end up the same way. Good fortune you was with them, mister. And that we was here, too. We belong with them and they with us. Back home in Shelterville. They don't belong out here. You do, I guess. But not with them.'

Steele sat easy in the saddle between the unconscious girl and her father, her father's friend and her friends. Having committed himself to a course of action but unsure how much further he was prepared to go along a path that promised nothing beyond the transient pleasure offered by the nubile body of an inexperienced girl. Certain, in fact, of only one thing—that if it had been anybody but her father who punched Sara Yancy in the face, he would have killed the attacker.

'Who are you, anyway?' Jonas Yancy asked, resentment spreading across his bristled features, reducing rather than displacing the anguish. 'And what's a man like you doin' mixed up with a bunch of crazy runaway kids?'

The youngsters were still shaken by the suddenness and violence of the Indian attack and by the additional shocks of John Carter's death, Al Yancy's wounding and the assault of Yancy against his daughter. Phil Shelby and Veronica Carter seemed on the point of sending angry retorts toward the man: but then discovered they lacked either the energy or the will to protest.

'Name's Adam Steele,' the Virginian supplied evenly. 'Some of these people weren't too proud to admit they needed some help. So I helped.'

'You don't look like the helpin' kind, Steele,' Yancy growled. 'Not unless it gets you somethin' you want real bad. Me and Doug showin' up here this mornin' keep you from gettin' a piece of what you're after?'

'Could be, feller.'

Yancy had expected a denial and prepared himself to counter it with an accusation that Steele was a liar. The soft spoken admission left the big man dumb-founded. But rooted him to the spot for just a moment. Then he powered forward, work-knarled hands clawed to grasp at the Virginian's leg, intent on hauling him down off the horse.

The move was telegraphed and unsubtle, planned in rising anger and executed in full-fledged rage. By a man who had ridden long and hard and then had to play his part in beating off the Indian attack. A man who was exhausted physically and drained mentally. An elderly man who normally was probably in good shape for one of his age. But who this morning was in worse shape than at any other time in his life, maybe.

So that it was simple for the younger, fitter, more mentally and physically alert man astride the stallion to slide his booted foot from the stirrup and lash out with it to the side. So the instep of the riding boot crashed across the throat of Jonas Yancy and sent the man sprawling out on to his back with a cry of alarm and pain.

'Weren't no call to do that, mister!' Douglas Carter accused bitterly, dropping down on to his haunches beside Yancy as the injured man writhed and rolled, clutching with both hands at his throat as he gasped for breath and his eyes bulged large. 'You could have gotten outta his way no trouble at all. Old man like him.'

He tried to prise the man's hands away from the injured area to take a look, but Yancy refused to let go: was perhaps afraid that the agony would get worse and his windpipe close up altogether if he did so.

Steele ignored both the men and all the youngsters except for Sara as he dismounted, dropped to his haunches, lifted the unconscious girl gently in his arms and draped her carefully over the saddle. Then he walked away, staying at the side of the stallion, one hand on Sara's sloping back to hold her in position while the other led the horse by the bridle.

'Where you takin' her, Steele?' Phil Shelby yelled, his tone as angry as the several pairs of eyes which the Virginian sensed were staring at his back.

'A place where we can do some talking is all,' Steele replied. 'What happens then will depend on what Sara says.'

'She ain't told you she wants to go, mister!' Douglas Carter shouted. 'If she don't, then this is kidnappin'!'

The Virginian glanced to the side, at where Sara was slumped limply over the saddle, her attitude and the way her flesh moved under the tight fitting shirt and pants emphasising the slender and yet totally feminine curves of her body.

'Reckon you could say she's napping,' he muttered through clenched teeth. 'But a kid she sure isn't any more.'

CHAPTER EIGHT

THE GIRL remained unaware of what was happening to her for perhaps thirty minutes, as Steele led the horse along the trail which followed the north bank of the Snake River. Walking directly toward the rising sun and never looking back over his shoulder. Breathing the clear, not yet warmed air of early morning and peering impassively out over the enormous tract of empty land that offered him a promise of peace which he did not believe.

Then Sara Yancy groaned her intention to regain consciousness and he came to a halt and lifted her down from the horse. The trail ran between the river and a stand of timber just here and he carried her into the trees and set her down under one of them, between the vee of two exposed roots and with her back against the trunk. He was squatting down in front of her, holding a canteen with the top off when she shook her head, vented a small cry of pain and raised both hands to touch the ugly bruise on her jaw.

'Hurts like hell, uh?' he said softly.

She opened her eyes, frowning her fear as for part of a second she failed to recognise his voice: then for an entire second stared into his face without comprehension.

'You want to take a drink of water?' he added, holding out the canteen toward her. 'It'll help get rid of that terrible taste you've got in your mouth right now.'

She had identified him before he started to ask the second question. So that the fear drained out of her which left her mind totally free to entertain other emotions. She cried, dropping her hands away from her jaw and pressing them tight against the tree roots to either side of her. Then she pulled her legs up to her breasts and interlocked her fingers around them: dropping her head forward to lean her brow on her knees. The sounds of her weeping grew less and soon her shoulders stopped shaking.

Steele moved away from her and sat on the root of another tree, waiting patiently for the girl to bring herself under control: having to keep his own instincts on a tight rein. For he had a powerful urge to return to her and take her in his arms. To comfort her, or for a far more selfish reason? It was because he did not know the answer to this question that he forced himself to remain at a distance of ten feet from her.

'Why did you bring me here, Adam?' she asked suddenly.

Steele jerked his head around to look across at her, surprised by the even tone of her voice. She continued to sit as before, hands clasped around her legs and head bent to rest on her knees.

'You all right now, Sara?' he wanted to know. 'Do you want that drink? Or some cooler water right out of the river to bathe that bruise?'

'No thanks. I shouldn't have spoke to my Pa the way I did. I deserve to feel as bad as I do. For a long time to come. Why did you do it, Adam?'

'Bring you here?'

'Yes.'

'For this.'

'What?' She was suddenly very afraid again and jerked up her head to stare at him: then showed a great relief in her big green, tear-ravaged eyes when he remained unmoving on the tree root.

'Talk, Sara,' he told her, a little tensely. 'Unless you think maybe enough's been said already.'

'No!'

'What else?'

Sunlight shafted down through the foliage of the trees, its warmth pleasant but its brightness harsh in the way it emphasised the discoloration and distortion of the bruise on the girl's face and the raw redness of the eyelids.

'I'm not ready, Adam. That's all. Not here and now. I thought the world of Johnnie and he's dead. Horribly dead. Just a few minutes ago. I've never killed anyone before this morning when I shot down that Indian. I ain't never spoke to Pa like that and he ain't never so much as lifted a finger to me until . . .'

'No sweat, Sara,' Steele interrupted and got to his feet. He jerked a thumb. 'The wagons and the people from Shelterville are back that way.'

'Adam!' She tried to rise but made it only halfway before she groaned and collapsed, her legs weakened and her sense of balance disturbed by the long period of unconsciousness. By the time she had recovered sufficiently to be able to locate the Virginian and bring him into focus, he had swung up into the saddle. 'You're not gonna leave me here?'

'Reckon I am.'

'But out here anythin' could happen. What if I can't . . .'

'Your head'll be clear in a minute or so, Sara. And if you don't rush right at the start, you'll be able to walk without tripping over your own feet. Then you'll be able to run. I didn't hurry bringing you this far. You should be able to get back to your friends in ten, maybe fifteen minutes. Nothing will happen to you in that time.'

'Take me back, please?'

'No. That's not the direction I'm headed in.'

'Well wait here with me, Adam. They'll be comin' this way. We're near the trail, ain't we?'

'We're near the trail,' he confirmed. 'And I guess they'll come this way looking for you. So you can stay here in the shade of the timber. You'll hear them way off.'

He jerked on his reins to turn the head of the stallion.

'Adam!' she shrieked, fear powering her tone to a high pitch of shrillness. 'Don't leave me! Stay here with me! Or take me with you. If you have to! I'll be ready later! After I've gotten over the shock of what happened! You have to understand that I . . .'

'No!' Steele snarled, halting in the act of heeling his horse forward. Then wrenching his head around to glare back over his shoulder and down at where Sara Yancy had made it to her feet now. Was having to lean hard against the trunk of the tree to keep from collapsing again. He forced his voice to maintain an even tone. 'There's nothing I have to do, Sara. For you or for anyone else.'

Now he did urge the stallion into movement, through the fringe of timber and out on to the trail, steering him into a left turn. Then, just before he demanded a gallop from the horse, he heard Sara burst into tears once more. And had to fight the urge to hold back his mount and listen to her: but knew that if he did so, he would weaken in his resolve and go back to her.

For more than a mile he rode the horse to the limit of the animal's speed, struggling to lose from his mind the sound of her weeping. Eastwards along the north bank of the shallow, narrow Snake, then crossing over the river when a great shoulder of rock forced the trail to swing to the south. But he ignored the ford as such, and rode along the centre of the river, welcoming the spray from under the pumping hooves as the droplets of water were thrown up and cooled the sweat beads which oozed from every pore on his face.

Then he slowed from the headlong rush, where the Snake entered a broad gully and ran faster, down a long incline: white and noisy where rocks littered the bed. He climbed down from the saddle and walked for a while, leading the horse by the reins along the bank. Then the gully ended and he saw the town in the far distance. Sat down on a water smoothed boulder which at this time of year was more than six feet from the river's edge and shaded his eyes by pulling his hat brim lower over his brow to peer at the cluster of buildings which crouched on the green landscape a good fifteen miles away.

His vantage point was probably a thousand feet above the town and the lush plain upon which it was sited: which gave him a bird's eye view of the two-street community and the scattered farmsteads which surrounded it. And he looked at the scene for a long time without really seeing it at all: for his mind was concerned with what lay behind rather than in front of him.

He had been a fool, of that there was no doubt. But then he always had been, as far as women were concerned. In the distant past maybe not so much. But recently?

Steele had invited all kinds of trouble into his life when he allowed himself to fall for the rich bitch Prudence Bancroft down in New Orleans. Then there had been Felicity Engle aboard the *Queen of the River* sternwheeler and Caroline Keyes at the ghost town of Rain. He had not fallen for either of them, but they had certainly been women and they had been around when trouble struck. Then there was quite literally a whole wagonload of trouble when he became tied in with Satan's Daughters.

There had been others before any of these. Hell, a whole town filled with widows at Borderville. Before those revenge-bent women? He shut his mind to such a distant past and did not allow himself to admit the reason for this until the name of Renita rushed again out of his memory. She was the reason for everything he had thought, said or done since he walked off the San Francisco waterfront, away from the warehouse in which her bullet riddled body was sprawled.

Thinking now of other women was merely an exercise in self-deception which was doomed to failure. Just as his idiotic pursuit of a spoilt girl who was little more than a child had been a futile pretense—if he had ever really succeeded in deluding himself into thinking he loved Sara Yancy.

He stood up from the boulder and checked over the stallion.

The animal was now rested and showed no outward signs of damage from being pushed so hard and far—to escape from what?

The Virginian swung astride the horse and heeled him into an easy walk, following the south bank of the Snake this time, almost arrow straight down the slope to the side of the fertile plain.

To escape from the temptation he felt so strongly to possess the body of the girl he had left back in the timber. Which would have been rape had he given in to his carnal desires for never would he have been able to convince himself that Sara had invited his attentions—despite the many occasions when she had looked at him in that special way with those child-woman eyes of hers. Despite, even, the way she had taken the initiative in kissing him at first light this morning.

Sara Yancy was more child than woman and she had been playing a childish game by trading on the woman in her. And for a long time Adam Steele had been so intent upon acting out his fantasy he had not been aware that she was also making believe. It had been easy for her, full of the bravado of youth and feeling secure while surrounded by her friends.

Did he ever really think of that girl as anything other than a piece of tail who might or might not prove something to him about his feelings for another piece of tail? That was all Renita was. A whore in the cantina of a Mexican village who gave herself to the Virginian while she was pretending to be a woman who had been taken before by only one man.

Could Steele hate her for that? Not for being a whore, but for pretending she was not a whore when she gave him her body. Because, until Renita, he had made it a point never to go with a whore. And if he did not hate her for tricking him, could he continue to love her in spite of it. And would he know, one way or the other, before he had taken the body of another woman? Any woman? Of any age?

He rode into town just after sundown and saw from the

signs above certain of the stores and other business premises that it was called Oakdale. From the western edge of the plain he had been riding a trail that sometimes followed the course of the Snake and sometimes did not. When evening came it was better when the river swung away from the generally straight trail because the warm, moist air close to the Snake was host to a million flying, biting midges which the ill-humoured Virginian found almost as irritating as his confused thoughts about a dead whore possessed by countless men and a girl who was doubtless a virgin.

He never got the better of the midges and so rode in off the trail with a face marked by many disfiguring red lumps which were painful to the touch of his gloved fingers. Which undoubtedly contributed to his bad temper as he angled his horse across the intersection at the centre of town and thudded a fist on the door of the livery stable.

'Come in why don't you?' a man called brightly. 'You know it's open.'

All Steele had known about the livery was that it was probably attended, for strips of lamplight showed at the base and sides of the door. He swung to the ground, lifted the latch and led the stallion inside.

'How would I know that, feller?' he growled.

'Oh, you're a stranger in Oakdale? Gee I'm sorry. It ain't often folks see strangers around here. Let me take care of your horse, uh.'

The man was about forty. Tall and broadly built. Running to fat around the middle and with a thick padding of excess flesh at his upper arms and thighs. He had jet black hair on his head, from his throat to his waist and beneath his armpits. Also on his forearms. He wore only a pair of denim pants. He had a round, pleasant, deeply bronzed face with many smile lines at the corners of his eyes and to either side of his mouth. He was smiling now, showing rows of fine, white teeth but there was a strangely disturbing stare in his dark eyes.

'You'll have to pardon me, being dressed—undressed, the way I am. But I was just about to bed down for the night.'

As the man advanced on him, Steele realised what was so strange about the vacant stare in the dark brown eyes.

'You can take care of horses, being the way you are?' he asked.

'You're a very observant man, mister. When I'm in my own place there ain't many can tell I don't have sight. Yeah, I can take care of horses very well. But if you don't trust me with your horse, mister, you can see to feed and water and currying. I'll just charge for rent of the stall and whatever he eats.'

He was not offended by the inference that the newcomer lacked faith in his ability. Which made Steele feel even worse about the implication.

'He's all yours, feller. I'll just take this.'

'Call me Jimbo, mister. Everyone does. That's a rifle you just slid outta the boot. You take it if you've a mind. But ain't no need to carry firearms around Oakdale. We don't never have none of that kinda trouble. Unless, of course, strangers bring it in?'

'Attached to the rifle is all, Jimbo. Every place else in this town looks to be closed up for the night.'

'Yeah, way it is out here. Folks rise early so they go to bed early. But Pete Lyons'll open up the saloon you bang loud enough on the door.'

'It's a room I'm looking for.'

'Pete's got them as well as liquor and beer, mister. He'll be as happy to rent you one as I am to take care of your horse.'

'Grateful to you.'

'You're welcome. I'll get the door.'

He wanted to display his skill in moving about the livery stable and he moved quickly and smoothly. Surprisingly so for such a big man. Almost incredibly so for a man who was blind. He avoided bumping into the stallion and Steele with the same ease as he curved around the paraphernalia of his business which had probably been littering the livery for weeks, months or even years. And he grinned directly into the Virginian's face as he ushered him across the threshold.

'I'm impressed, feller,' Steele said sincerely as he stepped out on to the street.

Jimbo shook his head and dropped the grin. 'Sorry, mister. I shouldn't boast like that. But then a guy like me can't do much he can be proud of.'

He slammed the door closed, as quick to dive into depression as he had been to soar to joy. And, feeling sorry for somebody else now, rather than having to control an impulse to indulge in self-pity, Steele ambled diagonally across the street to where the Oakdale House Saloon and Hotel stood, the only two storey building in town. He had time to thud a gloved fist on the door panel just once before a man called:

'Okay, I'll get it.'

Footfalls hit against floorboards and one of the double doors was unbolted and jerked open. Moonlight shafted over the Virginian's shoulder to bathe the man who stood on the threshold. A man dressed in a similar citified manner to Steele but in clothing that was a lot newer. The man so attired was clean and shaved and smelled of talc. He was about sixty, short and broadly built with a very red, round face under a sheened, hairless skull. There was a smell of whiskey on his breath.

'Ah, good evening to you, fellow traveller!' the man greeted with drunken enthusiasm. 'Come on in to this fine establishment and take some refreshment with me!'

'Reckon you're not Pete Lyons,' Steele said, stepping into the place.

Even after the drunk had closed the door there was enough moonlight entering through two big windows to show the basic geography of the room. It was large enough to have a bar running across the rear wall and half a dozen chair-ringed tables in front of this. There was also a stove in a corner. A door in back of the bar at one end of it was open. An aroma of reasonably fresh made coffee entered the saloon through that doorway: and captured Steele's attention despite the stronger saloon smells of stale tobacco smoke, liquor spilled hours ago, body sweat, cheap perfume and the breath of the drunk who had draped a hand over the newcomer's shoulder as soon as he closed the door.

'No, sir. That I ain't. Simmonds is my name. And liquor is my game. Come sample my wares.'

The stove was cold, perhaps had not been lit all day. But Simmonds had chosen the table closest to it. He tried to steer Steele in that direction, to where a valise stood open on the table and beside the bag was an uncapped bottle and a glass.

'Grateful to you, but I'm not a drinking man,' the Virginian said, extricating himself from the curve of the liquor salesman's arm. 'Need a room is all. Maybe some coffee if it's not too much trouble.'

Simmonds sighed. 'You not being a drinkin' man, that puts you in the fashion around this town, sir,' he growled miserably as he dropped heavily into a chair at his table and tilted the bottle to splash whiskey into the glass. 'Beer is about all they drink in the alcohol line. Enough to drive a man like me to drink!'

His broad shoulders began to shake and in his drunken condition there was a chance he might be starting to laugh or cry. It turned out to be gales of laughter which followed Steele as he went between a gap at the end of the bar and through the doorway in the rear wall.

'Evenin' to you,' a woman greeted, as a match was struck and its flame touched to the wick of a kerosene lamp. Above and to the right of where Steele stood. The woman who started down the stairway was in her mid-thirties, and looked pale and gauntly thin in the light of the lamp she held out in front of her. She had deep set, darkly bagged eyes, straight black hair and crooked yellow stained teeth. Contrasting with her plain face was what seemed to be a fine, full-bodied figure beneath the loose fitting white nightdress she wore.

'Help you, sir?' she wanted to know, her voice as dull as her eyes, when she reached the small hallway at the foot of the stairs.

'Room, ma'am.'

'I ain't married, sir.'

'Coffee. Something to eat and a bath if those wouldn't be too much trouble.'

'Bath we can't do sir. Get you a couple of jugs of hot water. Have to do best you can with the basin that'll be in your room.

'What I get paid for, sir.'

'Grateful to you,' he replied as she started back up the stairway and he trailed her.

'What I get paid for, sir.'

At the head of the stairway was a landing off to the left and right, with doors to seven rooms. The woman opened the door immediately across from the stairs and leaned in to set the lamp on a bureau.

'Ain't much, sir. But all you'll get in Oakdale. We don't get many folks passin' through in this part of the country. Hardly ever anyone stops over for a night. So Mr Lyons, he don't bother much providin' the comforts.'

The room was tiny and looked over furnished with a narrow bed, the bureau and a chair.

'It clean?' Steele asked.

'You got my word on that, sir. And I know on account of I do the cleanin'. Like I do most things around the Oakdale House. So you just let me know if there's any other little service I can do for you after you been fed and you got yourself washed up.'

As Steele stepped into the tiny room, the woman leaned forward, so that the twin mounds of her breasts brushed against his upper arm. They felt as firm as they had looked as she descended the stairway, restrained only by the fabric of the nightdress which had contoured itself to her flesh as she moved.

He pulled the door closed without looking back at her, then turned the lamp low and eased his body down on to the lumpy, blanket draped mattress of the bed. The springs beneath the the mattress protested at his weight and it was not until he was stretched out full length, gazing up at the pattern of stains on the ceiling, that he became aware his muscles were drawn as taut as the springs. Then, with his nostrils flared to the first trace of coffee scented steam which entered the room through the crack beneath the door and next the appetising aroma of frying bacon, he realised how much he needed a cup of coffee and how hungry he was.

And anger compacted into a tight, ice cold ball at the pit of his stomach. An anger he tried to direct at others but which he finally allowed had to be turned entirely inwards.

Both yesterday and today he had been every kind of a fool and he had no one to blame but himself. Yesterday a slip of a girl had made eyes at him and he had siezed upon an opportunity which had never really been there to use Sara Yancy as a palliative for what ailed him. Today he had discovered the truth of what he did and this caused him so much mental anguish he totally overlooked his physical needs. Which, because of the kind of life he had taken to living, could have got him killed. Which, in turn, was a good reason to feel angry at himself.

The woman with the gaunt and ugly face and the full and sensually curved body knocked on the door and came in with a tray on which was set a plate of bacon, beans and grits and a large mug of coffee, all of it steaming hot.

'I've put the water on to boil, sir,' she said as she put down the tray on the bureau. 'Be good and ready by the time you've eaten.'

Steele nodded without looking at her, then as soon as she had gone from the room he sat up, reached the tray down on to his lap and began to eat. He ate fast and without relish, to fill his belly rather than enjoy the food. Which was not his way. But then nothing about him over the past couple of days had been characteristic of him. Or very little, anyway. Very little during the past several weeks since he rode away from San Francisco. Not aware that he was mourning the death of a whore. So not knowing that he was searching for a cure for grief. Now disgusted with himself for being such a total fool.

The woman did not knock when she brought the two pitchers of hot water to the room. She set them down on the floor and Steele was certain he saw disappointment in her eyes when she picked up the tray of dirty dishes and glanced at him.

'Will that be all, sir?'

'What's your name, miss?'

'Marion, sir.'

'What is it you want?'

'Want, sir?'

'A man or the money a man will pay you, Marion?'

She scowled, then realised he could see her face clearly in the low light of the kerosene lamp. 'With a face like I've got, a woman learns to get along without a man. Has men, instead. Mostly them that are too drunk to care. You know what I mean, sir?'

'Could a man ever know?'

She shook her head. 'That's right. Men I don't care about. Just need the money they pay me. Mr Lyons ain't too generous, and I aim to get away from this town some day.'

'Put down the tray and close the door, Marion.'

'You mean it?'

He nodded and moved to one side of the bed, passing the Colt Hartford over his body to lay it on the floor. 'Reckon so,' he said with a sigh. 'About time to say what I mean again.'

'How's that, sir?'

'Talking to myself.'

'You want me to turn out the lamp, sir?'

'You're body as ugly as your face?'

'No!' she retorted sharply, then bit on her lower lip.

'Then leave the lamp. I've been stumbling around in the dark for too long.'

She showed a frown of confusion, then shrugged her shoulders, put the tray on the bureau and stooped down to reach for the hem of the nightdress. Steele looked at her nakedness as it was gradually displayed by the fisted hands raising the fabric: saw her body was as fine as it had promised to be, and felt a stirring of arousal in his loins.

'You got nothin' to worry about, sir,' she said when she had pulled the nightdress over her head and dropped it over the back of the chair. 'I keep myself as clean as the rooms. You know what I mean?'

'Do I look worried?' he asked.

She was at the bed in two strides, sat on it and swung up her legs. Then wriggled down until she was lying beside him, but not touching him. 'No, not worried I guess,' she said thoughtfully. 'But you look sort of strange, sir. Like . . . like . . .'

'Like what?'

'I don't want to make you angry..'

'You won't.'

'Like it was your first time!' she blurted out fast.

'It is,' he replied evenly. 'With a whore, for money.'

'I hope you won't be disappointed, sir.'

'I won't be,' he assured her. 'However it turns out, I'll know something for sure.'

'What's that, sir?'

'Whether I'm coming or going.'

CHAPTER NINE

THE WHORE was good at her trade. Adam Steele thought she was, anyway, within the limits of his experience. He was required to do nothing during the preliminaries to the act. And then, during the act itself, she was better than Renita had been. Which was all he needed to know. Comparisons with other women he had taken—or even had been taken by—were unnecessary. For it was the Mexican whore who had been influencing his thinking and his actions for so long. But would not do so after tonight.

The Virginian had not loved her.

As he lay in the arms of this whore, unable to see the ugliness of her face but pressed tightly to the length of her beautiful body—like an insecure child seeking reassurance from a mother—exhausted by the pleasure he had drawn from her and recalling vividly every word, every action and even every innuendo which had contributed to the near ecstasy he enjoyed, he experienced a great sense of relief.

He had loved what Renita had done to him and for him. Had been more effected by his coupling with her than with any other woman because, as a whore who was good at her trade, she had known what a man wanted and how to supply it.

This whore was even better. And maybe there were a thousand others in saloons and dancehalls and bordellos all over the country who were better still.

'You know something?' he said sleepily.

'What's that, sir?' Marion asked, holding his head to her breast and running her fingers gently over his cheek.

'I've been the biggest fool in creation where women are concerned.'

'Most men figure they're that, at some time or another,

sir. Did you find out that other thing you wanted to know about?'

'What was that?'

'Whether you're comin' or goin'?' She laughed and it was a very happy sound, revealing no hint that she was pretending to share in the Virginian's new mood. But then she had neither done nor said anything in any way to indicate that she did not reach the same pinnacle of passion that he did during the climax of the act.

'Tell you what,' he replied lightly. 'First I'll go to sleep. Maybe I'll come again later?'

He slept, falling asleep almost the instant he voiced his intention. Breathing easily and evenly. Not snoring. Naked and on top of the blankets.

When she moved away from him, doing all she could to try not to wake him, she was sure he was aware of what was happening. But she merely sensed this about the man. Saw no sign of it. She covered him with the blankets, then folded his hurriedly discarded clothes and stacked them neatly on the bureau. After this, she donned her nightdress and stood beside the bed looking down at his head on the pillow for some time.

They had talked little together and much of what he had said to her she did not understand. All she knew about him really was that she had pleased him. Given him a quite unexpectedly good time and made him forget whatever was troubling him. For a time or maybe for all time. Which meant she had done a good job. The best she had ever done? Hell, it could be the poor lonely guy would consider she was worth the bundle she had found in the hip pocket of his suit pants as she folded them. The bundle which she now formed into a roll and pressed into the empty coffee mug before she lifted the tray and carried it out of the room.

The Virginian slept on, content with the minor luxury of the lumpy mattress after an exhaustingly long day in the saddle topped by those last frantic few minutes in the arms of the skilled whore. Smiling briefly from time to time, like a man without a care in the world.

He did not hear the heavy footfalls of a man on the stairway and was completely oblivious to the approach of the liquor salesman until the door of the room swung open. He came awake fast then, aware of someone in the room who was not Marion. Fearful for part of a second as he failed to feel the familiar rosewood and metal of the Colt Hartford in his hands. Then rectifying this in a flurry of action—flinging himself, blankets and all, off the mattress and on to the narrow strip of bare floor between the bed and the wall under the window.

A man who had wanted to kill the Virginian could have done so then: as Steele wasted precious seconds extricating his hands from the blankets and then struggling to get the rifle out from under him. To cock and aim it—at a pair of shiny boots below the cuffs of smartly creased pants which were all he could see of the intruder under the bed.

'Sir, what's wrong?' the man asked, fast and nervous. And Steele recognised the slurring voice of Simmonds. 'Are you having a nightmare?'

'Only when I'm awake,' the Virginian groaned and pulled himself up on to his haunches.

The liquor salesman saw the rifle and his round, florrid face showed deep shock: 'Dear God, you might have killed me!'

'Instead of which I probably saved your life, feller,' Steele answered, easing up on to the bed and draping a blanket around his shoulders.

Simmonds had brought his glass up the stairs with him. He emptied it at a swallow. 'What's that you say?'

'Next time you go through a door which isn't your own, you'll knock I reckon.'

'I sure will.'

'So what else can I do for you?'

'I thought I'd tell you.' He made to raise the glass to his lips, but remembered he had already emptied it. 'Marion.'

'I know about her.'

'That she's leavin' town?'

The tension which had filled Steele in the fiasco of his response to Simmonds coming into the room was gone. Now, as he recalled something the whore had said to him, his muscles began to draw taut again. He stood up and moved around the end of the bed to where she had stacked his clothes.

Mr Lyons ain't too generous and I aim to get away from this town some day. That was what she had said to excuse the fact that she was a whore.

Simmonds watched with eager curiosity while Steele checked through the pockets of his clothing: the Virginian certain of which pocket the near five thousand dollar stake had been in—but feeling in every one of them anyway. His expression gave nothing away about the result of the search and he did not hurry as he dressed—totally unconcerned by the presence of the liquor salesman on the threshold of the room.

'She took you for quite a bundle, I bet,' Simmonds said, disconcerted by the quiet resolution of the Virginian's actions. 'See, I've been comin' through Oakdale for a long time, sir. Hardly ever worth my while, but it's on my route, so I come. And Marion's always here, peddlin' her ass for whatever a man's ready to pay. But there's no rich folks around Oakdale and damn few men with more than a few bucks in their pockets who ride through, I guess. But always Marion had this idea that some day she'd strike it rich. Said the day that happened, she'd walk right out on Pete Lyons, there and then. Marion's told me that a hundred times, maybe. So when I just saw her leave the hotel, dressed and with a valise, I figured you were in trouble, sir.'

'I'm grateful to you,' Steele said as he put his hat on and canted the Colt Hartford to his shoulder.

'You're welcome,' Simmonds said, stepping away from the

doorway to allow the Virginian out. 'Quite a bundle she took, uh?'

'Something over four and a half thousand dollars, feller.'

'Hot damn! You carry that much around with you? What are you, a bank robber or somethin'?'

'Nothing like that,' Steele rasped as he started down the stairs. 'I earned that money and a little bit more by not killing a man.'

Simmonds had made to trail him, but decided to remain up on the landing. For a while, at least. As he tried to make sense of what he had just been told. But he never would, for he knew nothing of the planned assassination which Steele had caused to fail, and the stroke of good fortune which had led to the Virginian collecting exactly the same amount as he was promised for the murder he never committed.

The Virginian did not hurry down the stairway, through the door, out from behind the bar and across the saloon. Simmonds said he had just seen the whore leave the hotel. Which probably meant she was still in town. But even if she were long gone, a few minutes would not make much difference. In country such as that which surrounded Oakdale, he would have little difficulty in tracking her.

Moonlight still filled the saloon. And outside came close to turning night into day—glinting on the glass windows, giving a white, phosphorescent look to the surface of the streets and causing the buildings to throw long, deep shadows. The buildings and the two Conestoga wagons which were parked, the teams still in the traces, in front of the livery across the street from the Oakdale House entrance where Steele stood. Stood and sensed heavy menace in the still, chill air of the night. The Colt Hartford canted to his left shoulder, since until the moment he stepped from the doorway, there had been no reason to expect trouble.

'Adam Steele!' a man yelled. From the moon shadowed doorway of a store next to the livery of the blind Jimbo.

The Virginian raked his impassive gaze in that direction and nodded imperceptibly. Not in response to the question. Acknowledging to himself that this was, indeed, his name, and so there was every reason to expect trouble. Wherever he was and in whatever circumstances.

'That's him sure enough, sheriff!' The confirmation shouted by Doug Carter who was inside the livery beyond the parked wagons. There was triumph in the tone of the silver-haired man.

'Toss that rifle out into the street and raise your hands in the air, Steele!' the lawman in the store doorway ordered. He sounded a little nervous.

The Virginian's pebble like black eyes moved constantly in their sockets, searching the outlines of the wagons, building façades and rooftops. Looking for Yancy and the kids and any deputies who might be out there hiding. He no longer felt like a fool and nor was he angry at himself. Or anyone else. Trouble was his business. He had decided to accept this fact after his experiences with Satan's Daughters and as he rode herd on young Jimmy Dexter from Mexico into California. He had made it so in Sun City and then in San Francisco. But had allowed his guard to drop since Renita made a fool of him: while he made a futile search for some other purpose to his life. Only to be tricked again by two other women.

A little more than forty-five hundred dollars was maybe a cheap price to pay for such an important lesson and so it was that he was able to put Marion completely out of his mind as he surveyed the main and the cross street of Oakdale. She would be no trouble at all.

'Why, feller?' he drawled into the hard silence which filled the cold night air after the sheriff had issued the command. He had seen nobody and heard no sound.

'Because you're under arrest, Steele! Charge of murder!'

'Who did I kill?'

'My Pa, Steele!' Phil Shelby called shrilly. He was in the livery stable, too. 'And you can't deny it!'

'Sheriff?'

'Yeah, Steele?'

'It happened a long way from this town. And it was self-defence. You shouldn't get involved in this.'

'Don't tell me my job!' the lawman shouted in high anger. 'Do like I say, or I'll shoot you down for resistin' arrest!'

'Do it, mister!' a man rasped from behind the Virginian, the voice heavy with menace. 'You better, because I got a scatter gun on you.'

Steele turned his head slowly to direct his impassive gaze back over his shoulder and across the moonlit saloon to where a naked-to-the-waist man was leaning on the bar, shoulders hunched and right cheek pressed to the stock of a short barrelled shotgun with a flared muzzle.

'Reckon you're the owner of this place?' the Virginian drawled evenly, as the man pressed his elbows harder to the bartop and thumbed back the hammer of the shotgun.

'Right, mister. Name's Lyons. Same as the sheriff of Oakdale. Lester and me are brothers. And I'm his deputy.'

'Pete, you got him covered?'

'Sure have, Lester!'

'So do like I say, Steele!' the lawman yelled, his confidence boosted by the response of his brother. 'You don't have a choice! You gotta see that now!'

The Virginian turned his head to face front again and pursed his lips. A retreat back into the saloon and an escape out through the rear had been his only chance. For the streets were too broad, especially at their intersection where the Oakdale House was situated and all the moon shadows were on the other sides of them, covering Sheriff Lyons and whoever else had a gun aimed at Steele. The Virginian would have to move across at least forty feet of open, moonlight-bathed ground to reach the angle of a corner which was the closest place of safety to the saloon entrance. Too far.

'He said to drop the rifle, Steele!' Doug Carter snarled as the Virginian stepped away from the threshold of the saloon and started out across the street. Then, more anxiously: 'Sheriff, don't trust him!'

There was always the danger of a man being panicked into squeezing a trigger in this kind of situation. But Steele was prepared to take the chance. For at least the odds were better than a run for the corner had offered. The sheriff would certainly have shot at him then. Pete Lyons, too. Carter and Yancy if their Sharps rifles were to hand. Maybe Yancy's son and Phil Shelby. A fusillade of shots fired instinctively, at least one of which would surely have found the target.

But this way men had opportunity to think. While they looked at their enemy coming slowly forward instead of trying to make a fast escape. Still in possession of the weapon he had been ordered to surrender. But making no overt threat against them.

'Rifle's as important to me as my life,' Steele said as he heard the footfalls of Pete Lyons on the floorboards inside the saloon. 'Hand it into somebody's safe-keeping if I have to. Don't intend to toss it around on the street like it was some run-of-the-mill bought off the shelf Winchester.'

'You folks in the livery stay out of this!' the sheriff snarled, and showed himself by stepping away from the deeply shadowed store doorway. Tall and broad shouldered like his brother. But with a drooping moustache whereas Pete was clean shaven. Both were close to sixty years of age. 'We got him now. Ain't that right, Pete?'

'Sure have!' the second lawman of Oakdale said gleefully, moving out of the doorway of his saloon and quickening his pace to close in on the Virginian's back. 'Hell, when we have to be, we're real terrific at this kinda thing, ain't we, Lester?'

'Only the best there is,' the sheriff crowed, grinning broadly as he came to a halt and levelled a Frontier Colt from his hip toward Steele's belly. And thrust out his free hand, palm upwards and fingers splayed to receive the rifle. 'You seem like a man that's been around, Steele. You ever been arrested so fine and smooth?'

The Virginian pursed his lips as he started to bring the rifle down slowly from his shoulder, angling it away to the side as the sheriff held the grin in place, still filled with confidence that he and his brother were in full control of the situation. Which was being enacted before an admiring audience.

'Answer the sheriff,' Pete growled as he stepped up close to Steele and nudged him in the small of the back with the shotgun muzzle.

'Tell you fellers one thing,' the Virginian drawled, a split second away from once more putting his life on the line. 'I never have been taken in by a pride of Lyons.'

CHAPTER TEN

STEELE exploded a shot into the night sky, firing the Colt Hartford one handed when the barrel was about twelve inches down from his shoulder, his finger squeezing the trigger the instant his thumb had cocked the hammer. Frightening and confusing two elderly men who were the law in this small, isolated, peaceful town. Men who had probably never been in this kind of situation before—of getting the drop on a man accused of murder. Who derived childlike joy out of their triumph and just did not contemplate failure now that the process of arrest had reached this stage.

'What the frig?' Pete Lyons snapped.

'Hey!' his brother yelled.

Steele saw the sheriff snap his head to the side, instinctively looking in the direction the bullet had been fired. And made an educated guess that the other brother had done likewise: staked his life on this by powering into a whirl, taking a double handed grip on the frame of the Colt Hartford and swinging it like a whip.

'I told you!' Doug Carter shrieked.

'Pete!' the sheriff roared.

The Virginian's actions looked like those of a crazy man's as he made a desperate, apparently ill-conceived bid to preserve his freedom. But in fact it was as carefully planned as the time allowed. Based upon a premise which had been the foundation of many tactical moves Steele had been forced to make in the past—that a man who has never killed before will not do so for the first time without pause for thought: unless from blind panic.

In this instance, the Lyons brothers were afraid, but held back from the brink of panic by the knowledge that each might kill the other.

The rifle barrel slammed into Pete's neck and sent the bare chested man toppling to the street with a roar of pain. The shotgun fell from his hands.

Steele went to the street, too. But of his own volition, hearing the crack of Lester Lyons' Colt and feeling the slipstream of the bullet as it cut through the air a fraction of an inch from his temple.

'Don't!' the Virginian commanded as he halted his roll when his body was prone, elbows digging into the hard packed dirt and rifle held in both gloved hands, barrel angled up to draw a bead on the star pinned to the left shirt pocket of the sheriff.

Lester Lyons was very close to panic now. He had seen his brother take the tumble and heard the cry of agony. Pete could be dead. Or badly hurt. Or maybe just a little bruised. Lester could not spare the time to check. He had paused for thought and taken a first shot at Steele the moment there was no danger of a miss tunnelling into Pete's flesh. He had missed sure enough and the stranger accused of murder had suddenly, shockingly, got the drop on him. While he still had the Colt at only half cock.

The two men locked eyes and for an immeasurably small part of a second each was certain he was gazing at the instrument of his death. Then a door banged open and hooves beat at the ground. Steele wrenched his attention away from the lawman and saw a horse and rider lunge out of the blind man's livery. A woman riding a black horse which she steered into a sharp turn between the two Conestogas then heeled into a flat out gallop along the street that ran eastwards.

It was the whore who had stolen his bankroll and he knew he had to let her go. For now. As he looked back at the sheriff not a part of a second too soon. For Lester Lyons was getting accustomed to surprises and learning to handle them better each time: might have put a bullet into Steele if the Virginian had not returned his attention to him.

'Who wants to die, feller?'

The lawman showed bitter disappointment and seemed to be listening to the diminishing sounds of clacking hooves as the newly rich whore rode her mount out of town and on to the trail which led across open country. They almost faded from earshot when he said:

'I think maybe I've been told some lies.'

'Leave it, Pete!' Steele said harshly as he heard a sound he recognised as a man crawling carefully but far from silently over hard packed ground. 'You're just a deputy. Your brother's the big noise in Oakdale.'

The sheriff sighed and slid the Colt into his holster. 'Man's right, Pete. It's all been goin' too damn fast for me tonight. Maybe we should all take a little time to talk and listen before we do some wrong can't be righted.'

Steele got to his feet, trusting the sheriff and so chancing a glance around. He saw Pete Lyons was also in process of rising, five feet short of where his shotgun lay on the street, massaging his neck and glaring malevolently at him. And that the open doorway through which the whore had made her escape was becoming crowded with the diminished group of Shelterville people. The two men, the Shelby youngsters, Veronica Carter and Al Yancy eyeing the Virginian with much the same brand of emotion as the pained Lyons. While Sara Yancy seemed to be trying to transmit some tacit message to him, but gave up the attempt when she realised he was not in a receptive mood.

Elsewhere, beyond the scattering of people who had been directly involved in the incident, a few weary-eyed and curious townspeople had ventured out of their houses to discover the reason for the shouting and the shot.

'Go put some clothes on, Pete!' the sheriff growled. 'Ladies present. And then you can open up your place for business. Guess some of us could use a drink.'

The bare chested man looked as if he might pick up his

shotgun, but decided that the icy look in Steele's eyes was entirely for him and he hurried into his saloon empty handed. His brother ambled across to where the gun lay, stooped with an effort to retrieve it and glared at the handful of bystanders.

'Get back to your homes, you people,' he ordered. 'Excitement's over. This town is back to normal again. Me and Pete did our jobs fine. Just fine.'

The work weary, mainly older age group men and women who had thrown topcoats over their night clothing to come out on to the street nodded their mournful agreement with this. And then did as they were told. Steele had re-entered the saloon by then and was seated at a table, in process of ejecting the spent cartridge from the rifle and reloading a fresh one into the chamber.

'She get away with much?' Simmonds asked tentatively as he stepped out from behind the bar. He didn't sound drunk anymore.

'Enough,' the Virginian replied.

'You talkin' about Marion Greenhill?' the sheriff wanted to know as he came into the saloon.

'Sheriff, people like us don't enter drinkin' establishments!' Doug Carter called.

'So wait here in the doorway,' the man with the drooping moustache flung back over his shoulder. Then to Simmonds, who had made it to his former table. 'Sample your wares again, Larry?'

'Sure, Lester.'

The liquor salesman brought his bottle over to the table where the lawman had sat down opposite the Virginian Simmonds had already poured himself a glass of whiskey. Lyons raised the neck of the bottle toward his lips and asked of Steele:

'You mind me goin' first? We ain't used to this kinda trouble in Oakdale. Shook me up a little.'

'Hey, ain't I gonna get to sell anybody anythin'?' his brother groaned from the doorway in back of the bar. He had donned a black shirt with a shiny deputy's badge pinned to the left chest pocket.

'Coffee,' Steele responded.

'He ain't a drinkin' man, Lester,' Simmonds reported to the sheriff, who was now sucking from the whiskey bottle.

'Me and my people could use some coffee,' Doug Carter called from the doorway.

'Coffee!' the Lyons brother at the bar rasped irritably. 'How the hell am I gonna get rich sellin' cups of coffee?'

But he retreated through the doorway into the back of the place. As his brother set down the bottle with a sigh of satisfaction and wiped the back of a hand over his wet lips.

'You don't look like the same kinda people they are?' he said to Steele.

'What kind are they?' the Virginian answered with a query and glanced across the moonlighted saloon to where Doug Carter and Jonas Yancy stood on the threshold, arms akimbo and careworn, weary eyed faces expressing resentment. Each held his Sharps rifle, barrel canted down at the floor, between his armpit and the crook of his elbow. The five youngsters had not crossed the street to the front of the Oakdale House.

'Different from most!' Carter snapped. 'But not deservin' of scorn because we have chosen to forsake strong drink, tobacco, fornication and the pursuit of riches!'

'And require our children to follow the ways of their elders!' Yancy augmented.

'I was scornful toward you?' Steele asked evenly.

'What greater contempt could you have shown, mister?' Yancy snapped. 'You tried to take my daughter from me and lead her . . .'

'It was my mistake, feller,' the Virginian interrupted, his voice soft spoken and yet with a force that was capable of driving the angry man into silence. 'But there was no harm done.'

Cups and a pot rattled against each other as Pete Lyons carried a tray into the saloon from out back. 'You people'll have to come and get it for yourselves,' he growled. 'My waitress woman just run out on me.'

The sheriff snapped a thumb against his fingers as a memory flipped into the forefront of his mind. 'That whore steal from you, mister?' he asked.

The Virginian had risen from his chair and gone to the bar. 'She did, feller. Another mistake. Seems I can't do anything right lately.'

'You sure as hell can't, mister!' the sheriff snarled, knocking his chair over backwards as he sprang to his feet and drew the Colt from his holster.

'We got him!' Jonas Yancy yelled as he and Doug Carter slammed the stocks of the Sharps rifles to their shoulders and took aim.

'Oh, my goodness,' Larry Simmonds murmured and seemed suddenly stuck to his chair, hands hooked over the curved edge of the table.

Pete Lyons said nothing. He merely parted his lips to show a grin of relish as he saw Steele come to a halt at the bar, eyes squeezing tight closed for part of a second: then snapping open, expressing nothing of what he felt about his situation—covered by three guns, with his own rifle at least twenty feet away.

'No smart ass tricks this time, Steele!' the sheriff rasped. 'Now you put your hands high or I'll blast one into your back for sure. And I friggin' mean it!'

The Virginian had no doubt of the truth of this and he raised his arms before he turned to look at his captors. And realised he had come within a hairsbreadth of being backshot by the elderly lawman. For it was now obvious just how deeply Lester Lyon's pride had been hurt out on the street when the tables were turned on him in front of strangers and townspeople alike. It had been a great strain for him to fake nonchalance after that, and it seemed as if even greater demands were being made upon his self control to keep from exploding a bullet into the impassive Steele after this new turnabout.

'Toss me my scattergun, Lester!' his brother asked eagerly.

'Get it your friggin' self!' the sheriff retorted, and this stab of anger directed toward Pete acted to take some of the pressure off his emotional instability.

'Where's the money, Steele?' Doug Carter demanded.

Aware that the threat of imminent blasting death was passed, the Virginian was able to force his gaze away from the hard set face of the sheriff and vent a low sigh as his eyes switched between Carter and Yancy.

'What money?' he asked.

'The money you killed Eric Shelby for!' Jonas Yancy replied.

'Hold it, you people!' the sheriff cut in. 'This is my town and the prisoner's in my custody. I'll do the damn questionin'.'

Steele's mind started to race, but he forced it to slow down: to consider carefully everything that had happened since he first met up with the three boys and three girls around the Conestoga that was stuck in the mud.

'That's the way, Lester,' Pete Lyons urged as he started to move into an arcing traverse of the saloon, eager to have the shotgun back in his hands but aware of the danger of placing himself in the line of fire. 'Don't let these strangers walk all over...'

'And you shut up as well!' the sheriff shot at his brother without taking his level unblinking gaze off the impassive, unmoving Virginian. Then he lowered his voice to ask: 'Did the whore take the whole lot, Steele?'

'Everything I had in the way of money, feller.'

The man with the Colt moved his head slightly from side

to side and whistled through pursed lips. 'Then I guess that makes it the most expensive screw in history.'

'Give or take a few dollars, four and a half thousand,' Steele revealed.

'No!' Doug Carter blurted.

'Much more, sheriff!' Jonas Yancy added. 'The woman's probably in it with him! Yeah, that's it! He knew we was on to him and he used her to take the money outta town! It was twenty-five thousand and more, sheriff! Like we told you!'

'Well, mister?' Lester Lyons demanded, his tone as cold as his eyes. 'You admitted a while back you killed this Eric Shelby. Way the kids tell it, shootin' took place without witnesses. And you claimed Shelby's horse and everythin' that was on the animal. Which included, accordin' to these two guys, twenty-five thousand dollars of other people's money.'

'Stole from my bank!' Jonas Yancy augmented bitterly.

'By a man for who the town was partly named.' Carter growled with a wistful look in his weary eyes. Then he shook his head. 'And one everybody thought was too loco after his wife died to even know what day it was.'

'This ain't gettin' us nowhere!' the sheriff complained angrily. 'I told you people to leave it to me!' Again he did not take his gaze off the Virginian, wary of the dudishly dressed, dirty and unshaven man's apparent complete lack of response to what was happenig around him. And recalling the lightning reactions he had displayed a few minutes ago. 'Come on, Steele! You did see the wagons roll into Oakdale, didn't you? And you had Marion Greenhill take the loot away from here? Hell, she even rode outta the livery at just the right time!'

'Saddled her horse right in front of where we was standin'!' Jonas Yancy muttered.

'Wasn't just forty-five hundred she was carryin', was it?' Lester Lyons went on as his brother ducked under the aimed guns of Carter and Yancy and made a dash to snatch up his shotgun from the floor beside the sheriff's overturned chair. 'It was the twenty-five thousand this guy Shelby took from Shelterville and you took from him? You admit to that and tell us where you planned to meet up with the whore and it'll go easier for you at the trial.'

Steele, his shoulders beginning to ache from holding his arms above his head, ignored the grinning Pete Lyons and his grim faced brother to look at the men standing on the threshold of the saloon. 'Which of them was it?' he asked evenly.

'What?' Yancy said.

'Which of the kids told you the story?'

'Me!' Lester Lyons snarled, his rage mounting again. 'Talk to me, Steele.'

'All of them,' Carter answered. 'We was sure at first, when we rode outta Shelterville to find the children, it was them stole the money. Never did occur to us that poor crazy old Eric Shelby took it. But after we found Sara where you left her this mornin' and she told us about you killin' Eric . . . Well, mister, it made sense. Specially after we'd searched the wagons and not found no money. And all the children told the same story Sara did.'

'They tell you he fired the first shot, feller?' Steele asked.

'These people ain't doin' what you told them, Lester,' Pete Lyons growled.

'Sure they did,' Jonas Yancy supplied as Carter remained silent, a thoughful frown on his weary face. 'But that figures. Eric saw them wagons and thought he was being trailed by folks from Shelterville. Ain't many Conestogas like that around no more. So when he saw them he guessed right they were from . . .'

'Mister?' Carter cut across what the man at his side was saying.

'Yeah, feller?'

'I just thought of somethin'.'

'Well save it!' Lester Lyons snapped. 'I've heard enough

talk. Gonna lock this killer up in the gaolhouse and raise a posse to go after the whore with the loot. You can talk to him all you like through the bars of the cell.'

'About damn time!' Pete Lyons growled. And advanced on the Virginian, the shotgun thrust out menacingly in front of him. 'You hurt my neck, mister, but that won't be nothin' to what you'll feel when the noose . . .'

The Sharps rifle in Carter's hands cracked out a shot, deafeningly loud within the confines of the saloon.

'For the friggin' love of God!' the silver-haired man shrieked as everyone stared at him, then towards the spot on the table where Larry Simmonds' almost empty bottle of whiskey had stood. 'It was the children! The Goddamn children who . . .'

'Don't profane, Douglas!' Jonas Yancy shouted. 'You don't know what you're sayin'.'

'No, Pa!' Veronica Carter denied shrilly from out on the street. 'I swear it wasn't me.'

'Nor me, sir!' Al Yancy yelled. 'Or Trudy! I know Trudy couldn't have done . . .'

'Mr Carter!' Phil Shelby started.

'Adam!' Sara Yancy shrieked, the forceful power of her voice swamping the words the Shelby boy was bellowing. 'I didn't know! I though it had to be you!'

Steele heard her voice without being able to distinguish what she was saying to him. Because his life was on the line again. He had started the move even before she shouted his name. And had to channel all his concentration into the task of getting under the barrel of Pete Lyon's shotgun before the man could squeeze the trigger.

'Watch him, Pete!' the sheriff warned, fear and rage almost causing him to choke on the blurted out words.

He swung his gun as he spoke them, but was unable to get off a shot. Because the Virginian, his arms down now and pushed out in front of him, had lunged into the cover of Pete

Lyon's form—as the saloon owner snapped his head around from looking at the shattering effect of the rifle shot.

Pete did fire his gun. But by accident and too late to send the spreading shot pellets into his intended target. For Steele had made contact with him by then—thudded his shoulder into the flabby belly without allowing the jarring impact of the collision to interrupt the bent over run he was making. His arms encircled the bigger man's thighs and his gloved fingers became interlocked. Which enabled him by a slight straightening up from the waist to lift the suddenly cursing man off his feet.

Tables and chairs were sent tumbling in every direction as Steele forced his way among them: kicked over either by his own pumping feet or by Pete Lyons' as the angry and frightened man lashed and flailed with his legs.

It was as the frantic run came to an abrupt end, with the saloon owner's back being thudded into the front wall of his place, that the shotgun discharged its load. Spraying the lead pellets at point blank range into the face of Oakdale's sheriff: tearing into the man's flesh and ripping it from the bone, shredding the eyeballs and shattering the teeth. Removing, in just part of a second, enough tissue for the skull to show through the welter of blood, from the crown of the head to the point of the jaw.

Pete Lyons saw his brother's features disintegrate in this way as he started to slide down the wall the moment Steele backed away from him. The wind was knocked out of him by the way he had been crushed between the Virginian's shoulder and the timber wall. And there was such a searing agony in his back he was sure his spine was broken. His mind, already assaulted by frantic pleas from his punished nervous system was unable to accommodate the horror of seeing his brother die so violently. And plunged him into merciful unconsciousness.

Steele turned away from him and himself saw the terrible

effect of the shotgun blast—as the corpse of the sheriff folded backwards across an overturned table and then slid to hide its mutilated face against the sawdust strewn floor.

'I've done nothin' wrong!' Larry Simmonds shrieked from where he sat on the floor.

His plea of innocence was triggered by the fact that Steele happened to rake his eyes across the man's fear whitened face as he folded erect after snatching up his Colt Hartford. And the coal black eyes were ice cold, totally lacking in compassion for the dead sheriff. Or feeling for the people who were still dying. Out on the street. As a result of the fusillade of gunshots which had cracked out while the Virginian was charging across the saloon with his weighty, desperately struggling, shrilly cursing burden.

'Take it easy, feller,' the Virginian drawled as the gunfire was curtailed. 'I've got nothing against perfection.'

CHAPTER ELEVEN

THERE were four blood blossoming bullet holes in Douglas Carter's broad chest but he was a tough old man who possessed a great deal of willpower: and he was determined to hang on to the final vestiges of his life for as long as necessary to finish what he had started.

He lay, sprawled on his back, legs splayed and arms out straight at his sides, about fifteen feet from the doorway of the Oakdale House. The Sharps rifle he had wrested from the grasp of Jonas Yancy had been hurled far off to the right, in a fit of rage or a spasm of agony. But not before it had drilled a bullet into Veronica Carter's chest, with enough velocity to tunnel through her heart and burst clear of her flesh at the back.

'Just had the single shot in the rifle,' Carter croaked as Steele halted beside the close to tears Jonas Yancy and looked impassively down at the dying man. 'Fittin' I used it on my own thievin' daughter.'

'You stupid, friggin' fool!' Sara shrieked, dropping to her knees and beating at the ground with the sides of her clenched fists. 'You killed her for nothin'.'

It was Phil Shelby who had avenged the death of Veronica —and now hurled away his Navy Colt and ran to fling himself down across the dead girl, his frame wracked by sobs.

'No need to curse any more,' the Virginian drawled. 'Reckon you're all grown up.'

Douglas Carter had dismissed all the youngsters from his pain filled mind and directed his entire attention up at Steele and Jonas Yancy. He seemed to resent the younger man's interruption. 'Had to be them, didn't it, mister?' His eyes, starting to glaze over, moved in their sockets. 'Don't you see,

Jonas, old friend? We was right from the start of it. If this feller had killed poor old Eric on purpose and then stole the money, don't make sense he'd have stuck with the stupid wet-behind-the-ears children, does it? Not a man like he is.'

'Don't follow, Doug,' Yancy countered, his tone plumbing the depths of misery. 'Maybe he figured . . .'

'He's not listening, feller,' Steele cut in. 'He's dead.'

Yancy covered his face with his hands and shook his head slowly from side to side. 'God, what'll I tell his wife?' he groaned. 'Douglas, John and Veronica. All gone.'

'Two of them for nothin'!' Sara wailed. 'Can't you see, Pa? You and Mr Carter did search the wagons, like you said. And when you didn't find nothin' that's when it seemed like Adam had to have stole the money! But by that time one of the wagons was burned! The Carter wagon!'

'John?' Yancy gasped, dropping his hands down from his face. 'He took the money?'

His eyes made a frantic search of the faces of all the youngsters. Sara expressed full and embittered confidence in what she had said. Her brother, his head heavily bandaged where the Indian bullet had creased him, and Phil and Trudy Shelby, looked from her to Jonas Yancy and nodded their belief in what Sara had suggested.

Steele moved away from the centre of the street, and was met in the doorway of the livery stable by the blind Jimbo who was leading the black stallion, saddled and with the bedroll fixed firmly in place.

'Man doesn't have his sight, he gets compensated with other things, mister. Just knew that if you walked away from this mess, you'd want to ride away. Real fast.'

He demonstrated his skill again, by reaching out to place the reins accurately into the Virginian's free hand—the one not canting the Colt Hartford to his shoulder.

'I'm broke, feller.'

'I know. Marion paid for a whole night's stabling and feed

and water, mister. Also give me some money to pay for your hotel room. Pete make it, okay?'

'He did. His brother didn't.'

'Damn shame. Old Lester was always itchin' to make a big pinch. Guess you're gonna go after Marion Greenhill?'

'No, feller,' the Virginian answered, sliding the rifle into the boot and swinging up into the saddle. 'She earned what she took. But there again, if I happen to run into her by accident, it won't be an accident she dies from.'

He jerked on the reins to wheel the stallion.

'Adam!' Sara Yancy called.

He did not rein the animal in from its easy walk as he looked back at where the Shelterville people stood on the street beside two of their dead.

'We're goin' back home with Pa. It's the only way we can show it was John took the money from Pa's bank. Without none of the rest of us knowin' about it. Adam, there's so much I want to say . . .'

'Sara!' he shouted.

'Yes, Adam?'

'Just two things I want to say to you!'

'What are they?'

He could hardly hear her as he steered the horse east along the street, aware of many pairs of wary eyes watching him from behind the curtained windows to either side.

'Grateful to you, girl,' he muttered. 'And . . . GOODBYE.'*

** From this book. Adam Steele will return in the next title of this series.*